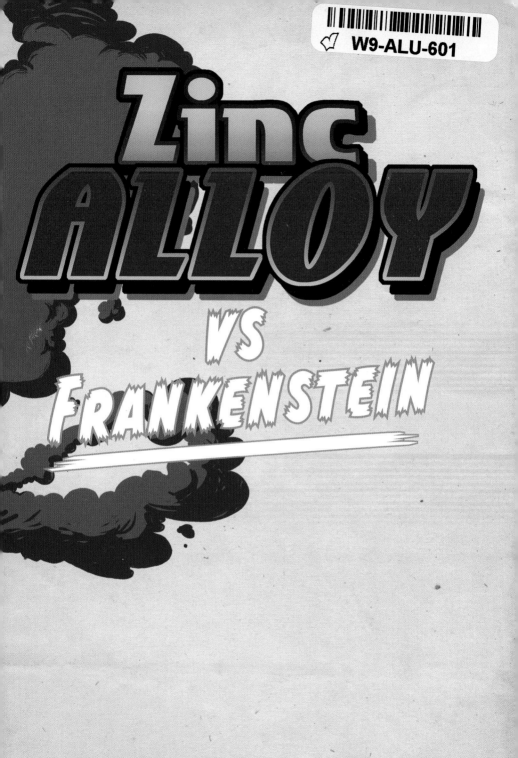

Zinc ALLOY

VS FRANKENSTEIN

STONE ARCH BOOKS
www.stonearchbooks.com

Graphic Sparks are published by Stone Arch Books
A Capstone Imprint
1710 Roe Crest Drive
North Mankato, Minnesota 56003
www.capstonepub.com

Library of Congress Cataloging-in-Publication Data
Lemke, Donald B.
Zinc Alloy vs Frankenstein / by Donald Lemke; illustrated by Douglas Holgate.
p. cm. — (Graphic sparks. Zinc Alloy)
ISBN 978-1-4342-1188-0 (library binding)
ISBN 978-1-4342-1391-4 (pbk.)
1. Graphic novels. [1. Graphic novels. 2. Heroes—Fiction. 3. Robots—Fiction.]
I. Holgate, Douglas, ill. II. Title.
PZ7.7.L444Zin 2009
741.5'973—dc22   2008032062

Summary: When a good deed goes bad, an angry mob chases Zinc Alloy out of Metro
City. To escape, he hides in a creepy, old house on the edge of town. But inside, the world's
newest superhero faces his most frightening challenge yet — robo Frankenstein! Can Zinc
survive against this two-ton terror, or will he become monster mush?

Creative Director: Heather Kindseth
Graphic Designer: Brann Garvey

Printed in the United States of America in North Mankato, Minnesota.
052015
008920R

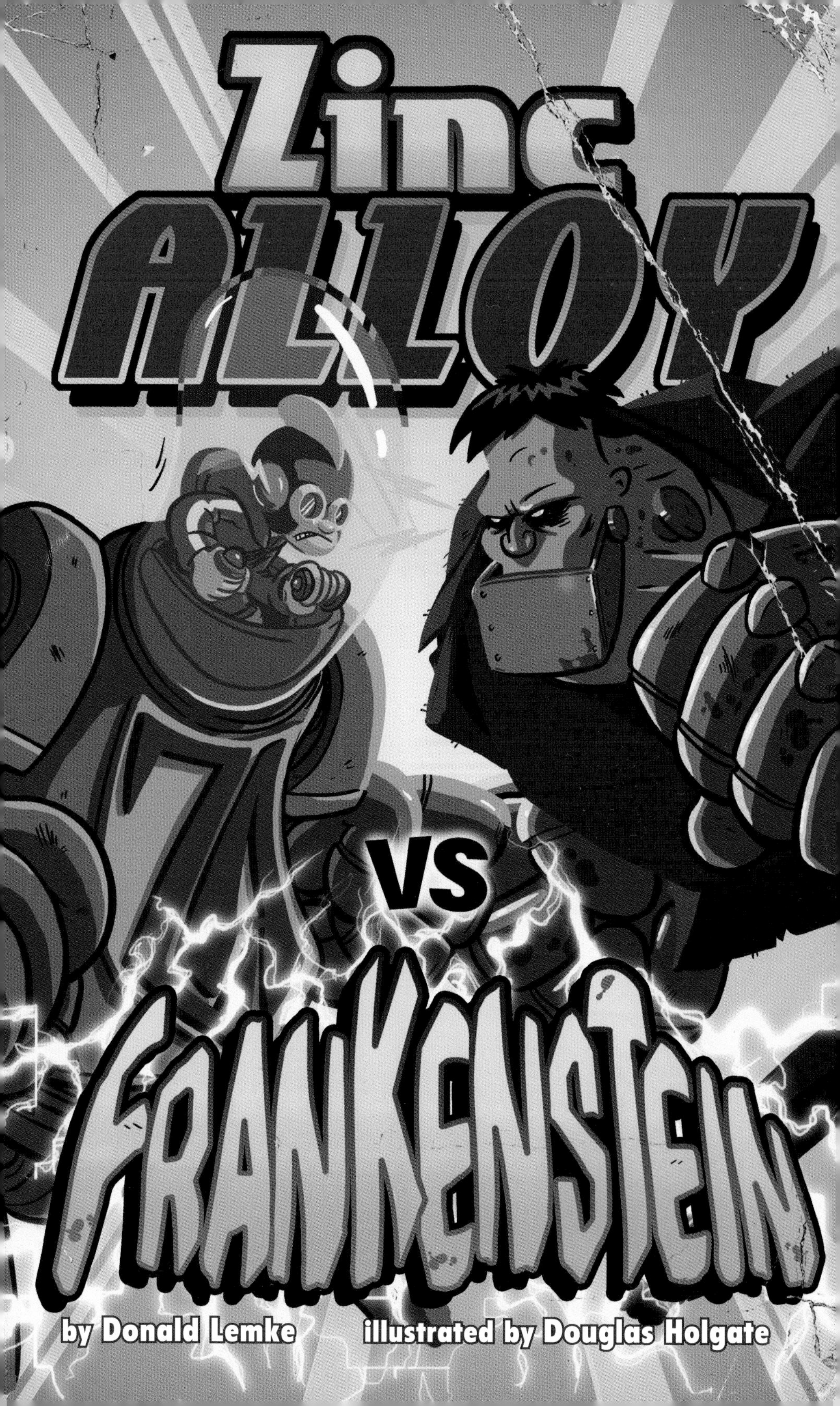
Zinc
ALLOY
VS
FRANKENSTEIN
by Donald Lemke
illustrated by Douglas Holgate

Cast of CHARACTERS

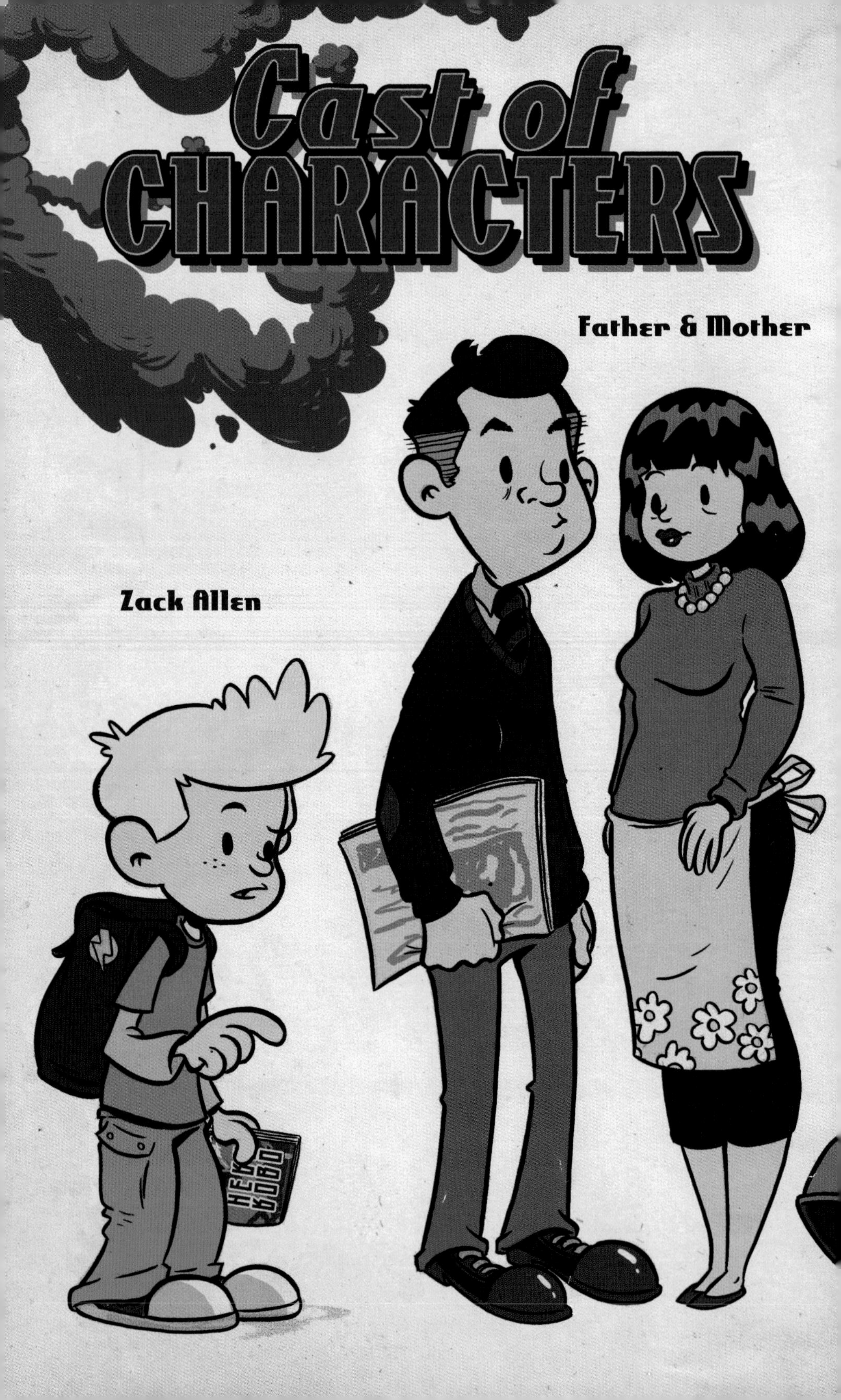
Father & Mother
Zack Allen

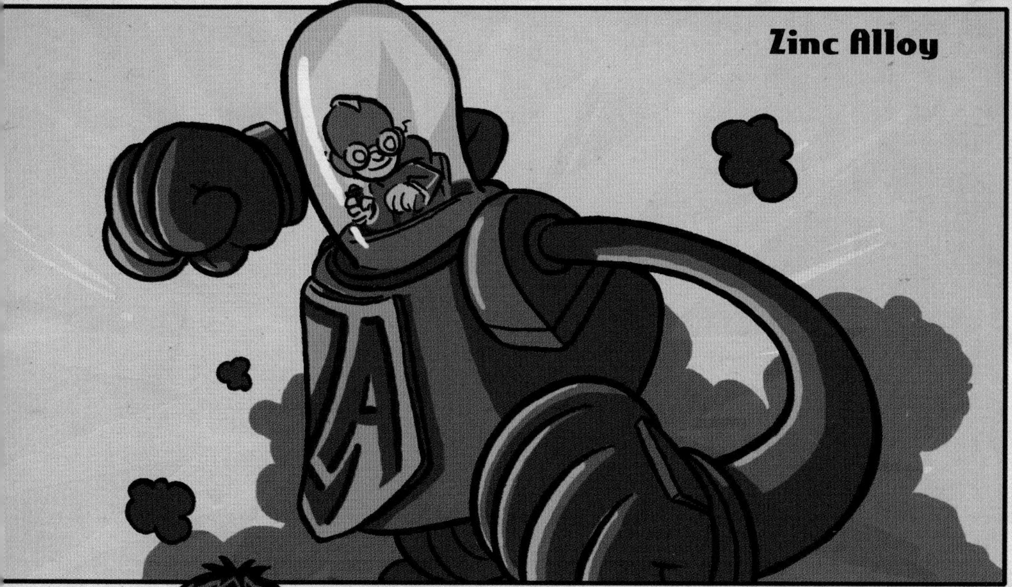
Zinc Alloy

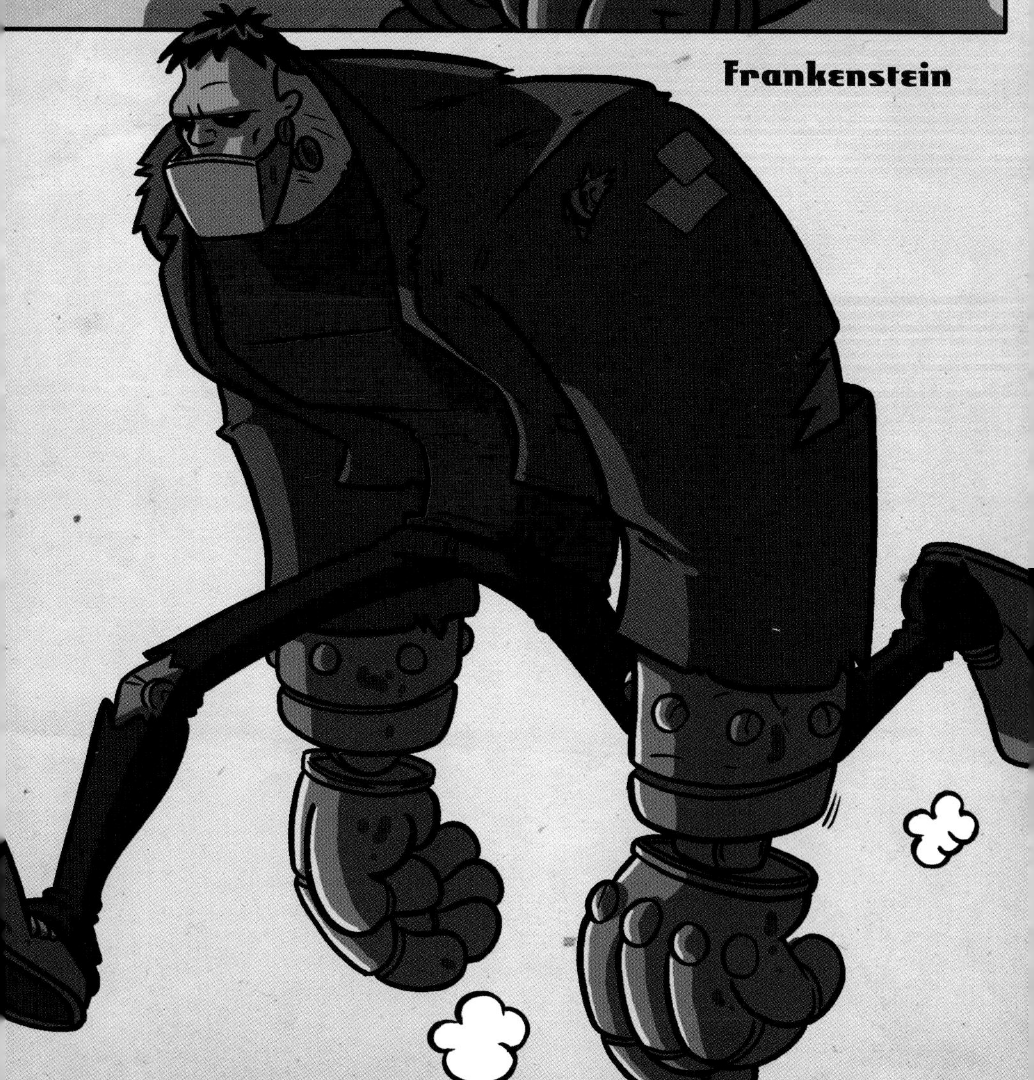
Frankenstein

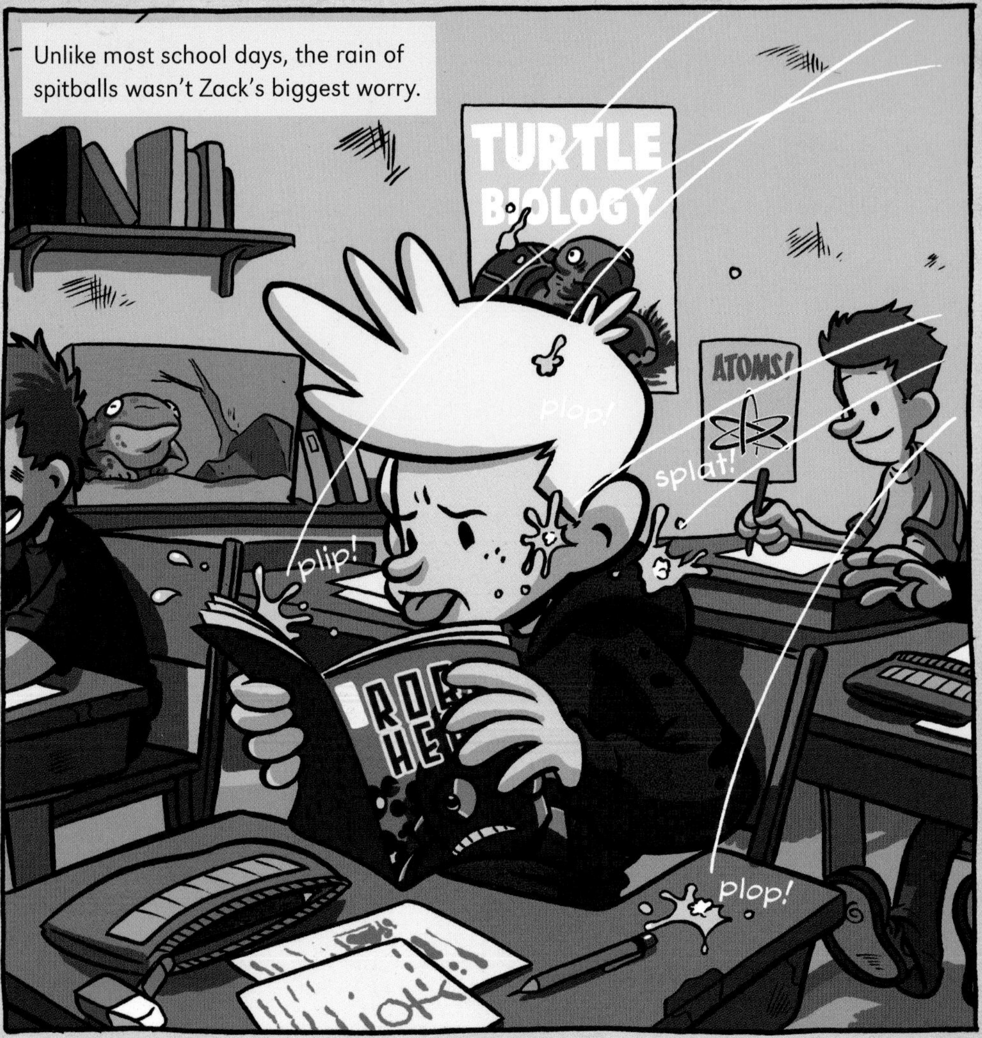
Unlike most school days, the rain of spitballs wasn't Zack's biggest worry.
TURTLE BIOLOGY
ATOMS!
plop!
splat!
plip!
plop!

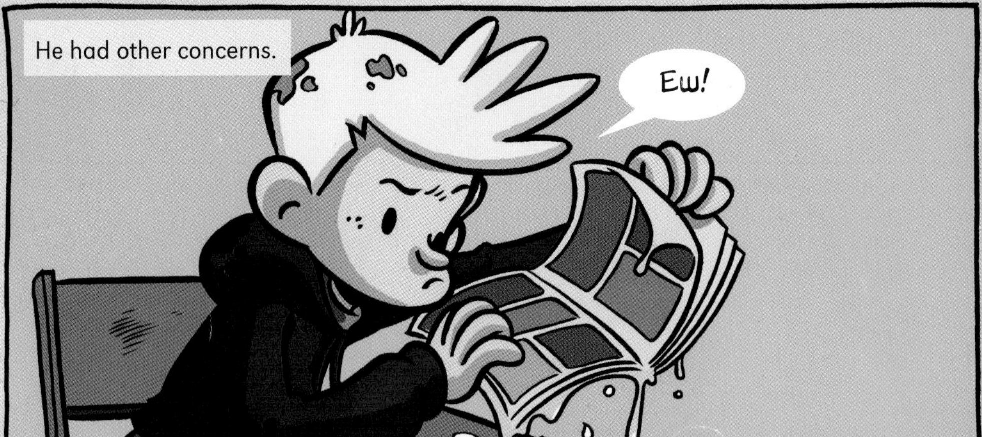
He had other concerns.
Ew!

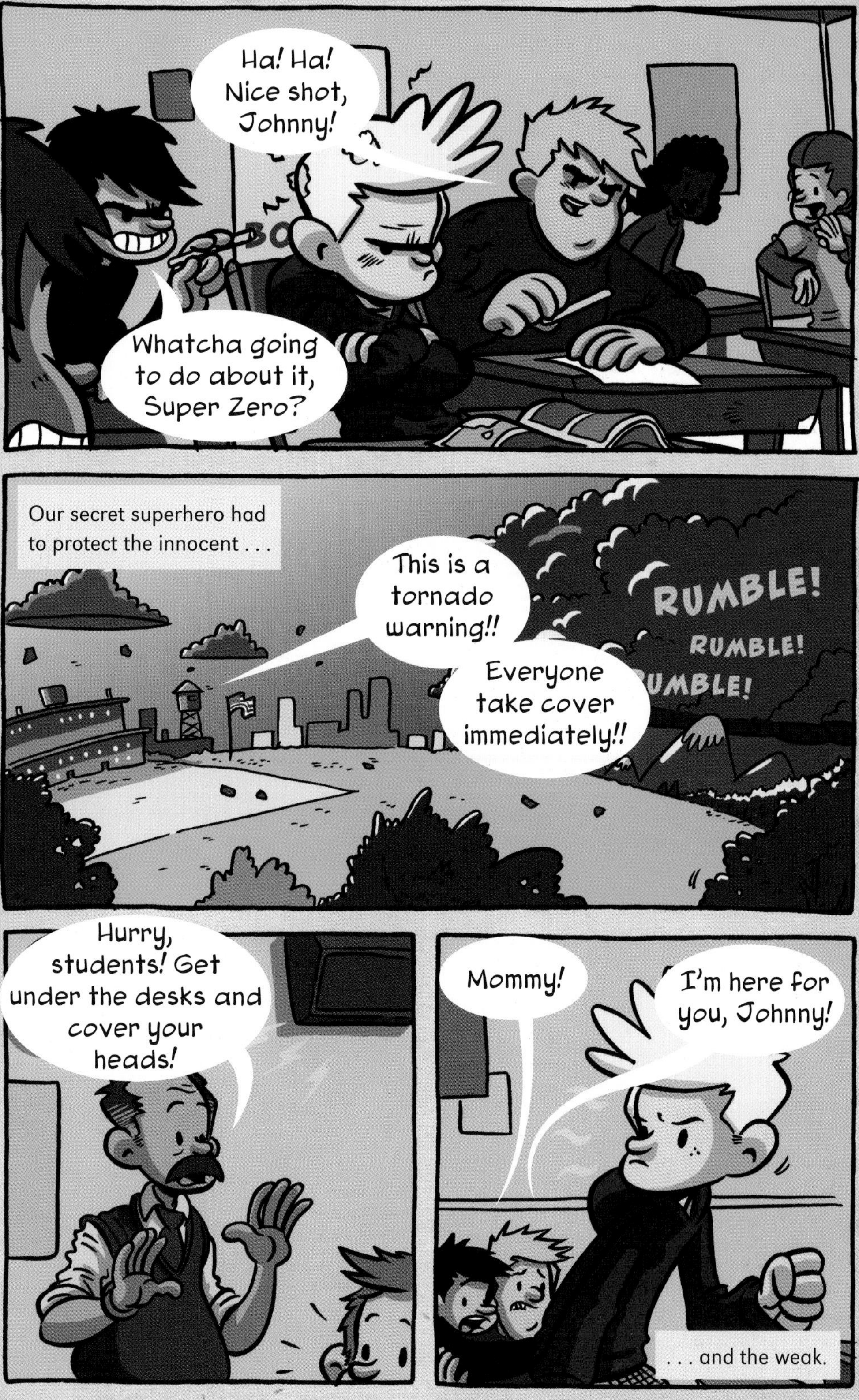
Ha! Ha!
Nice shot,
Johnny!
Whatcha going
to do about it,
Super Zero?
Our secret superhero had
to protect the innocent . . .
This is a
tornado
warning!!
Everyone
take cover
immediately!!
RUMBLE!
RUMBLE!
UMBLE!
Hurry,
students! Get
under the desks and
cover your
heads!
Mommy!
I'm here for
you, Johnny!
. . . and the weak.

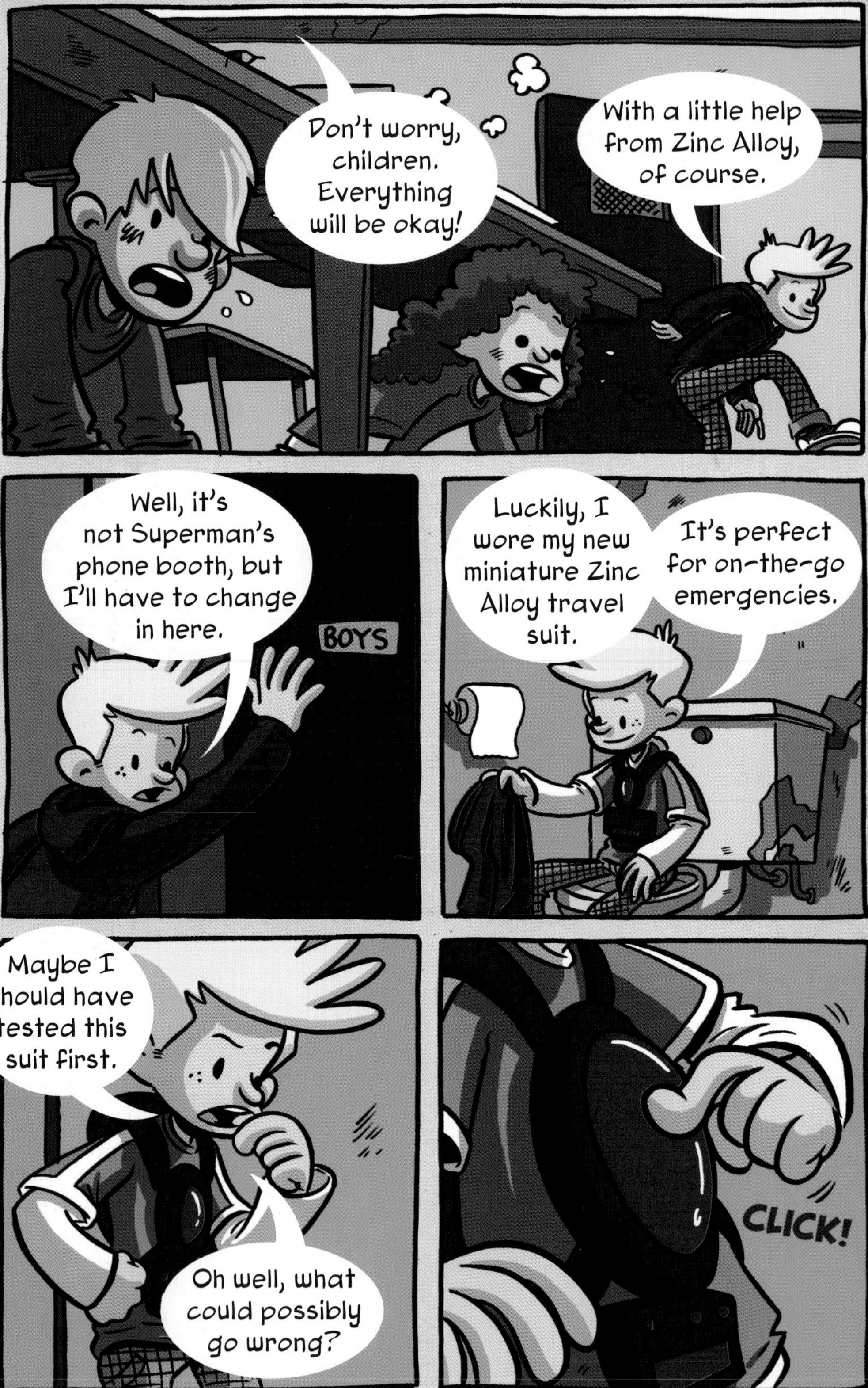
Don't worry, children. Everything will be okay!
With a little help from Zinc Alloy, of course.
Well, it's not Superman's phone booth, but I'll have to change in here.
BOYS
Luckily, I wore my new miniature Zinc Alloy travel suit.
It's perfect for on-the-go emergencies.
Maybe I should have tested this suit first.
Oh well, what could possibly go wrong?
CLICK!

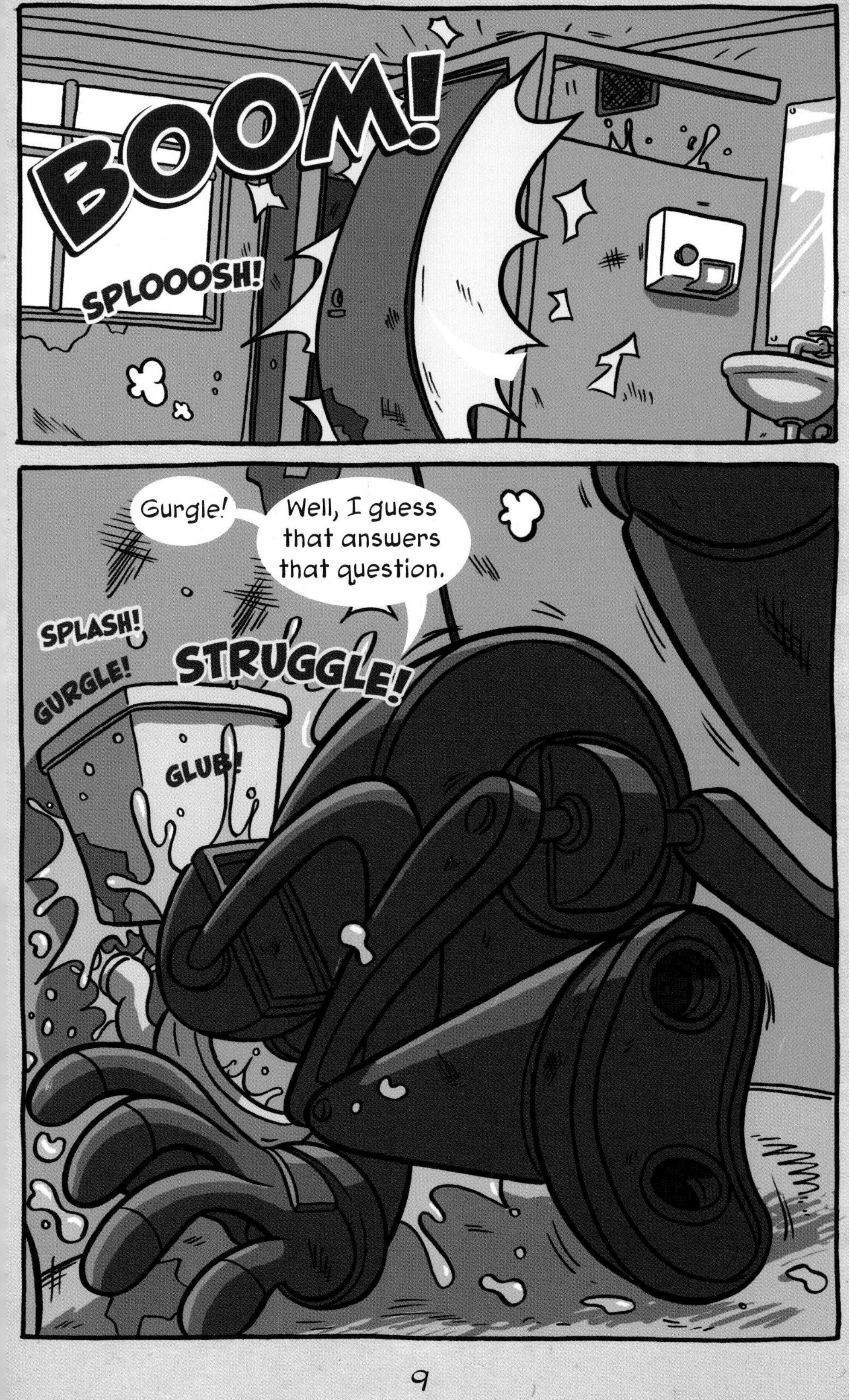
BOOM!
SPLOOOSH!
Gurgle!
Well, I guess that answers that question.
SPLASH!
GURGLE!
STRUGGLE!
GLUB!

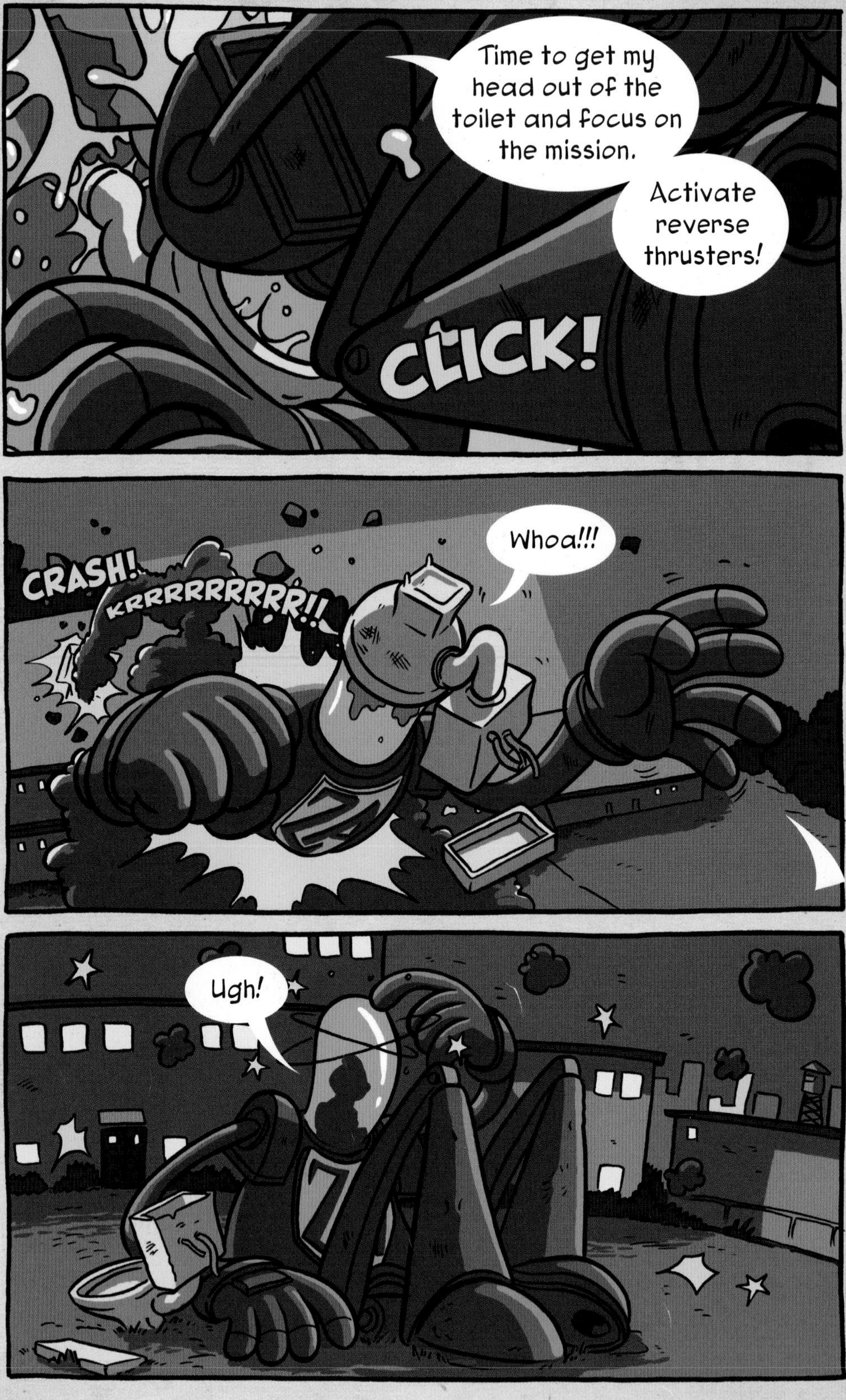
Time to get my head out of the toilet and focus on the mission.
Activate reverse thrusters!
CLICK!
CRASH!
KRRRRRRRRR!!
Whoa!!!
Ugh!

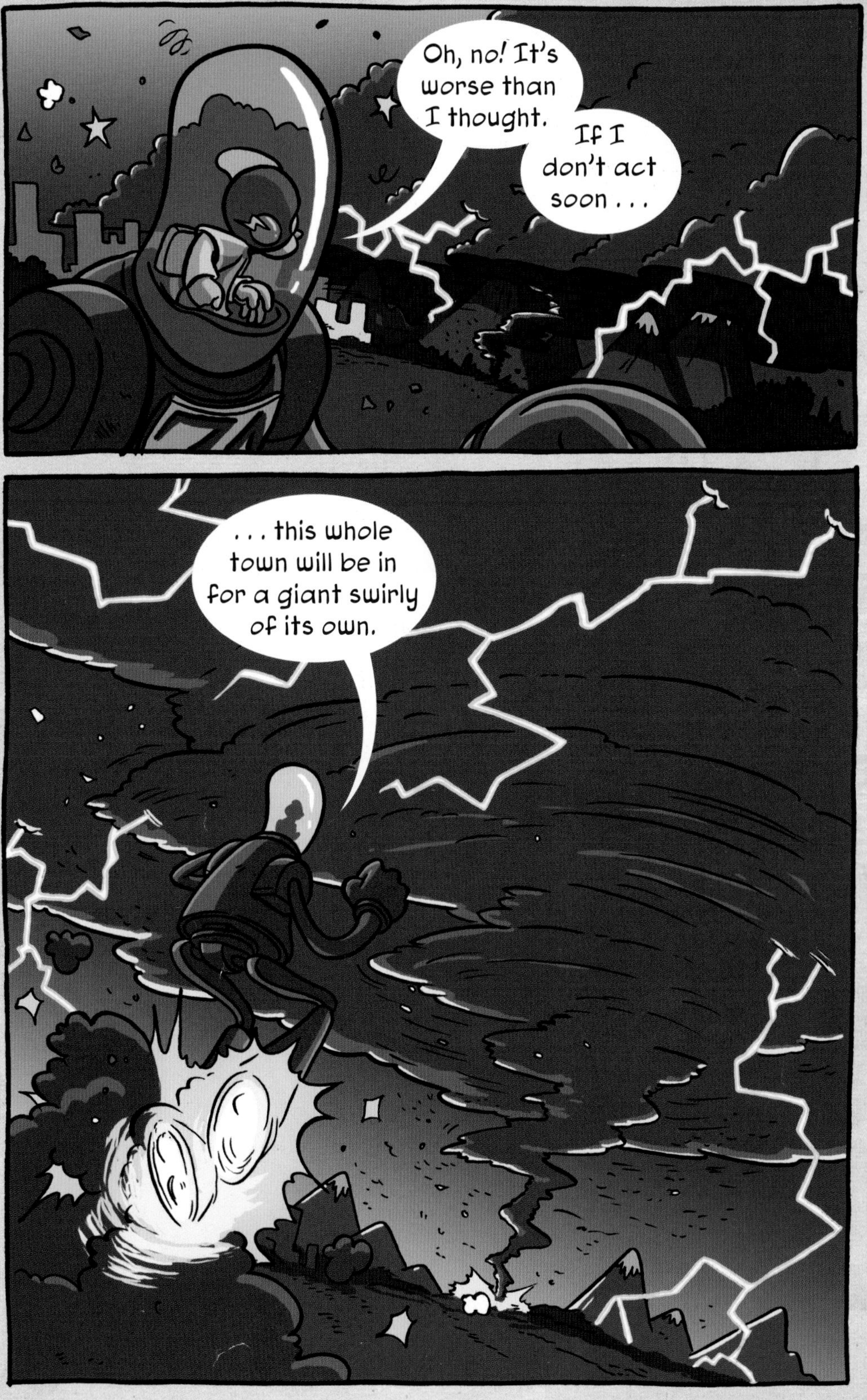

Oh, no! It's worse than I thought.
If I don't act soon . . .
. . . this whole town will be in for a giant swirly of its own.

Mortal men would cower in the face of such a threat.
But I, Zinc Alloy, have chosen this heroic life and fear is not an option.
I have vowed to defeat evil of any form. I have sworn to uphold truth and justice. I have —
Uh-hum! Excuse me, but I can't hold on much longer.
Oh, right!

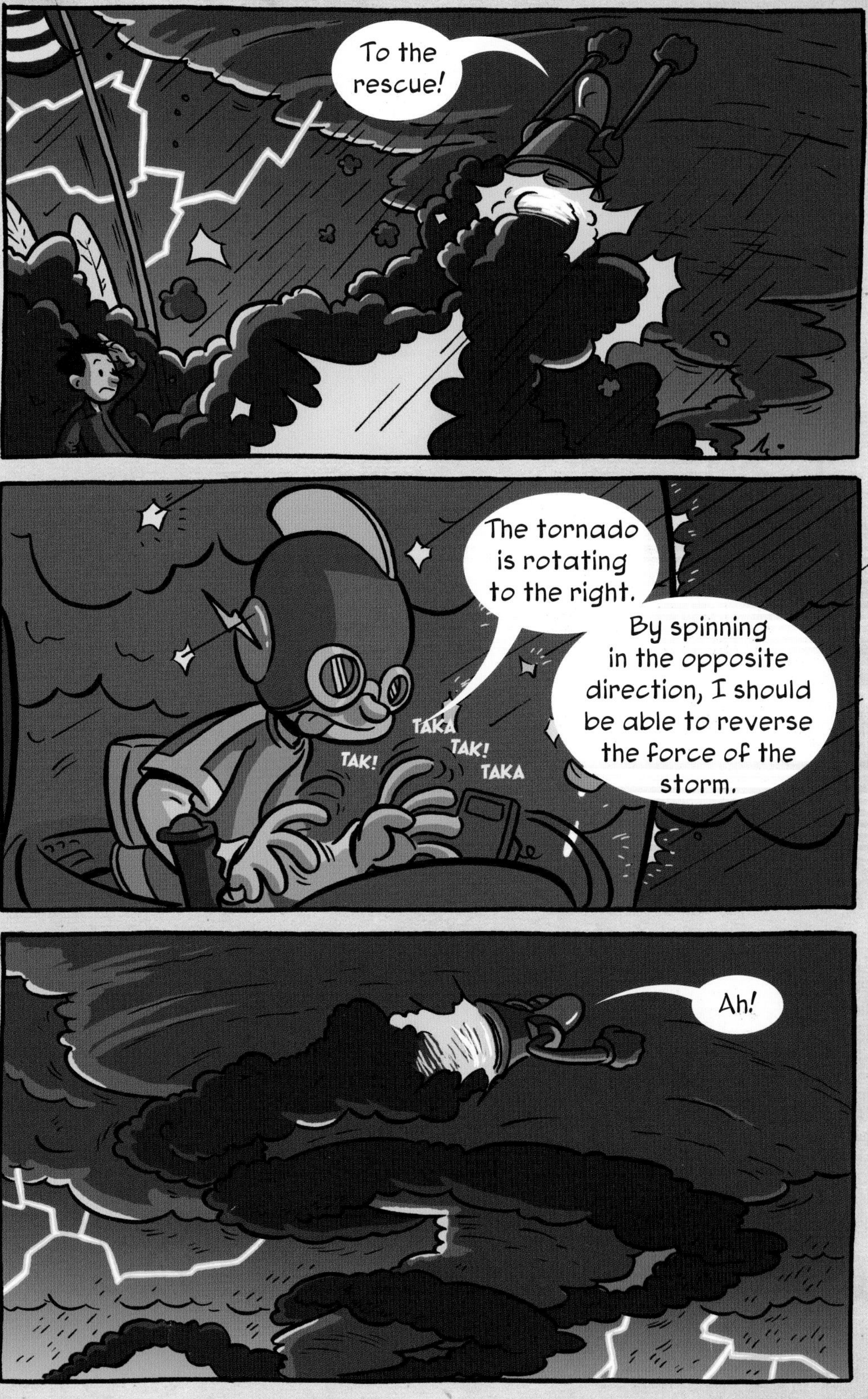
To the rescue!
The tornado is rotating to the right.
By spinning in the opposite direction, I should be able to reverse the force of the storm.
TAKA
TAK!
TAK!
TAKA
Ah!

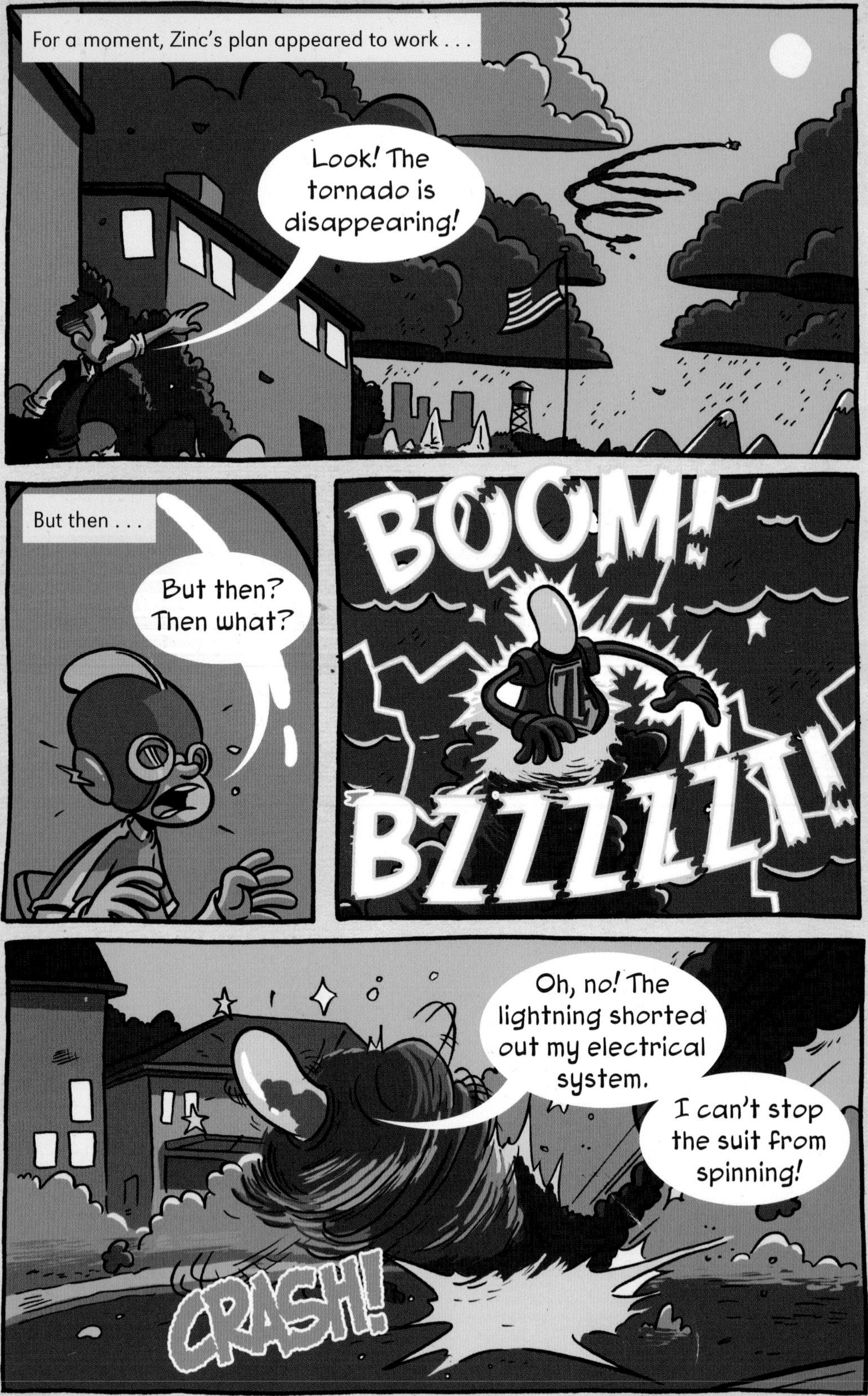
For a moment, Zinc's plan appeared to work . . .
Look! The tornado is disappearing!
But then . . .
But then? Then what?
BOOM!
BZZZZZT!
Oh, no! The lightning shorted out my electrical system.
I can't stop the suit from spinning!
CRASH!

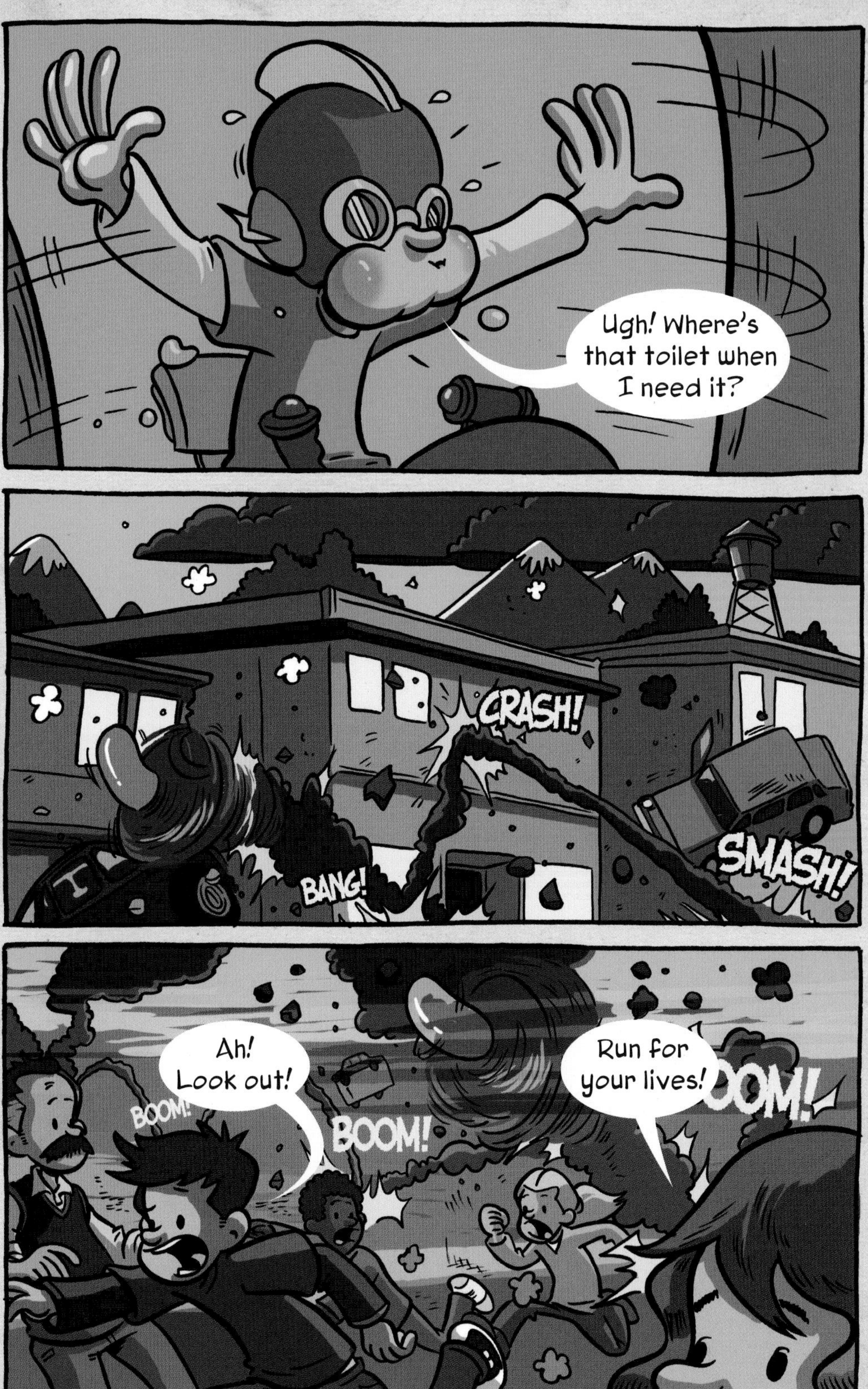
Ugh! Where's that toilet when I need it?
CRASH!
BANG!
SMASH!
BOOM!
Ah! Look out!
BOOM!
Run for your lives!
OOM!

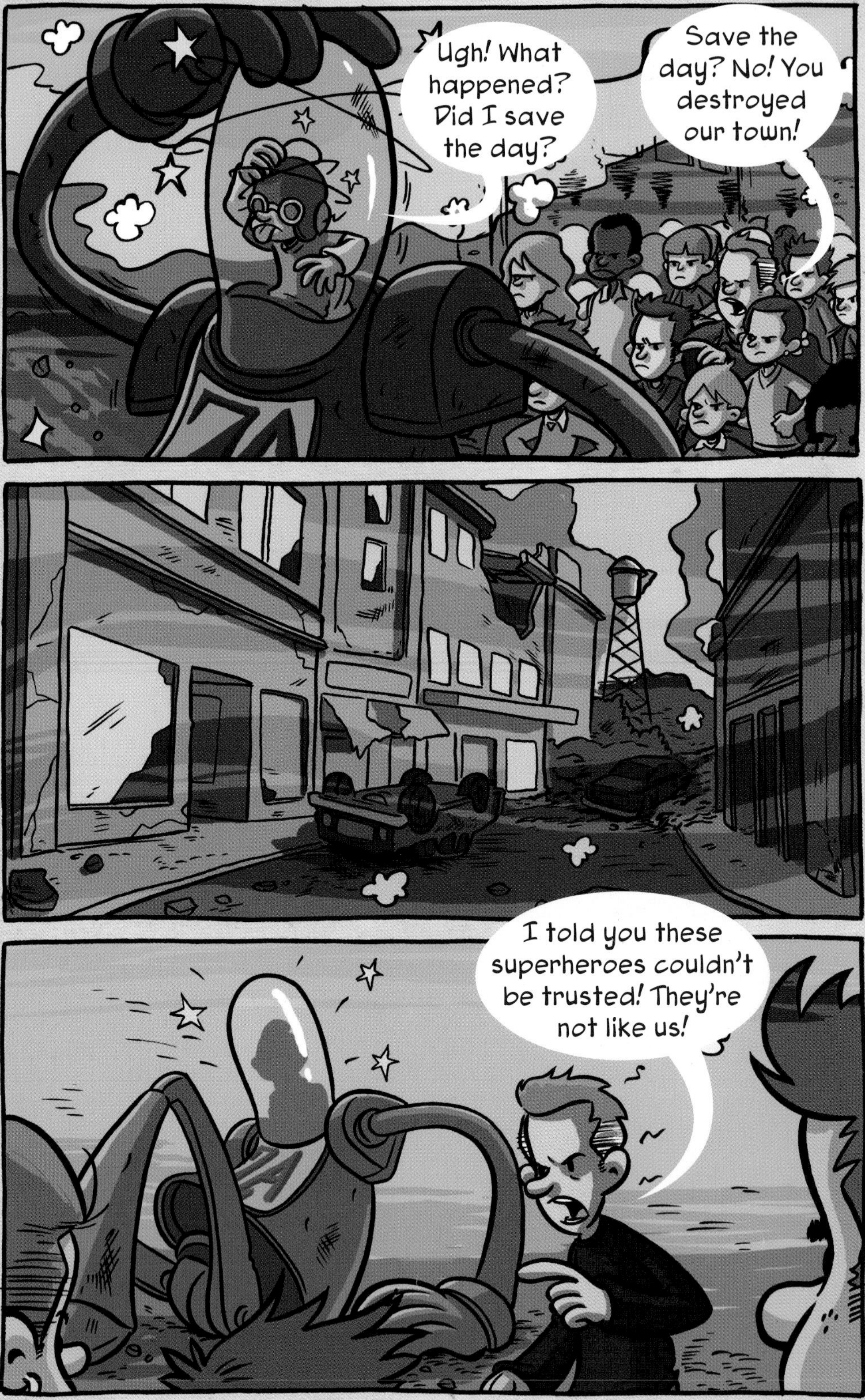
Ugh! What happened? Did I save the day?
Save the day? No! You destroyed our town!
I told you these superheroes couldn't be trusted! They're not like us!

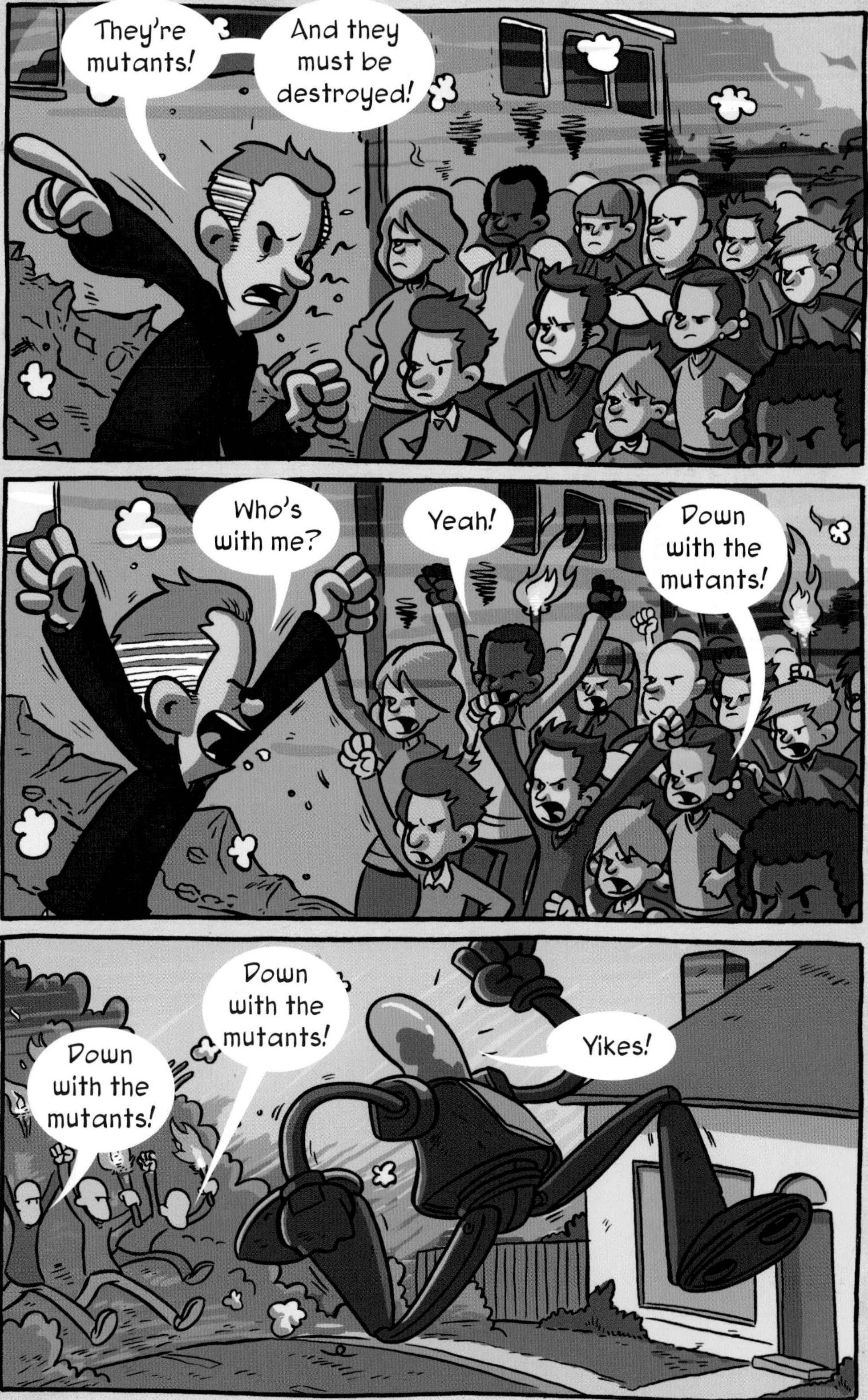
They're mutants!
And they must be destroyed!
Who's with me?
Yeah!
Down with the mutants!
Down with the mutants!
Down with the mutants!
Yikes!

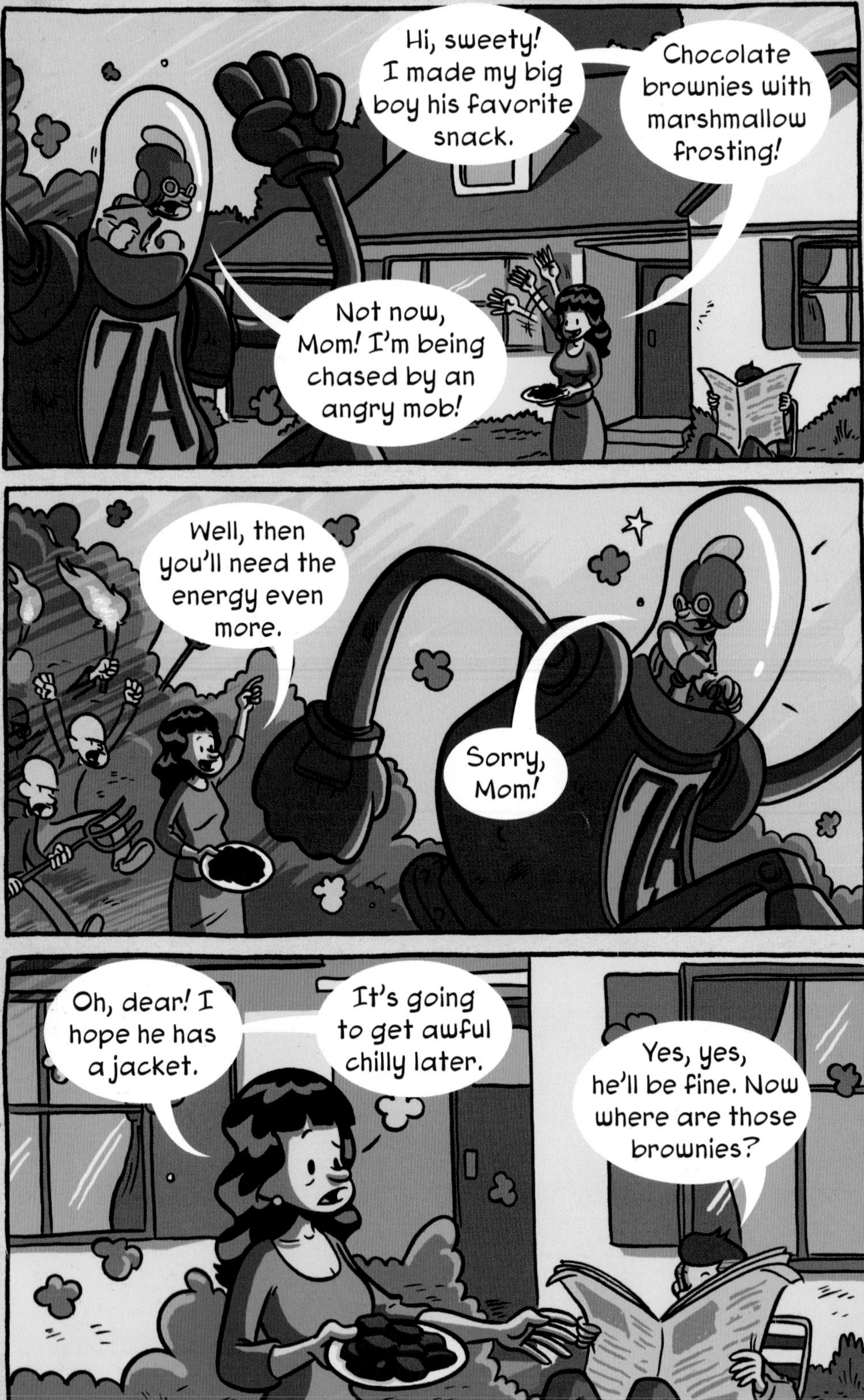
Hi, sweety! I made my big boy his favorite snack.
Chocolate brownies with marshmallow frosting!
Not now, Mom! I'm being chased by an angry mob!
Well, then you'll need the energy even more.
Sorry, Mom!
Oh, dear! I hope he has a jacket.
It's going to get awful chilly later.
Yes, yes, he'll be fine. Now where are those brownies?

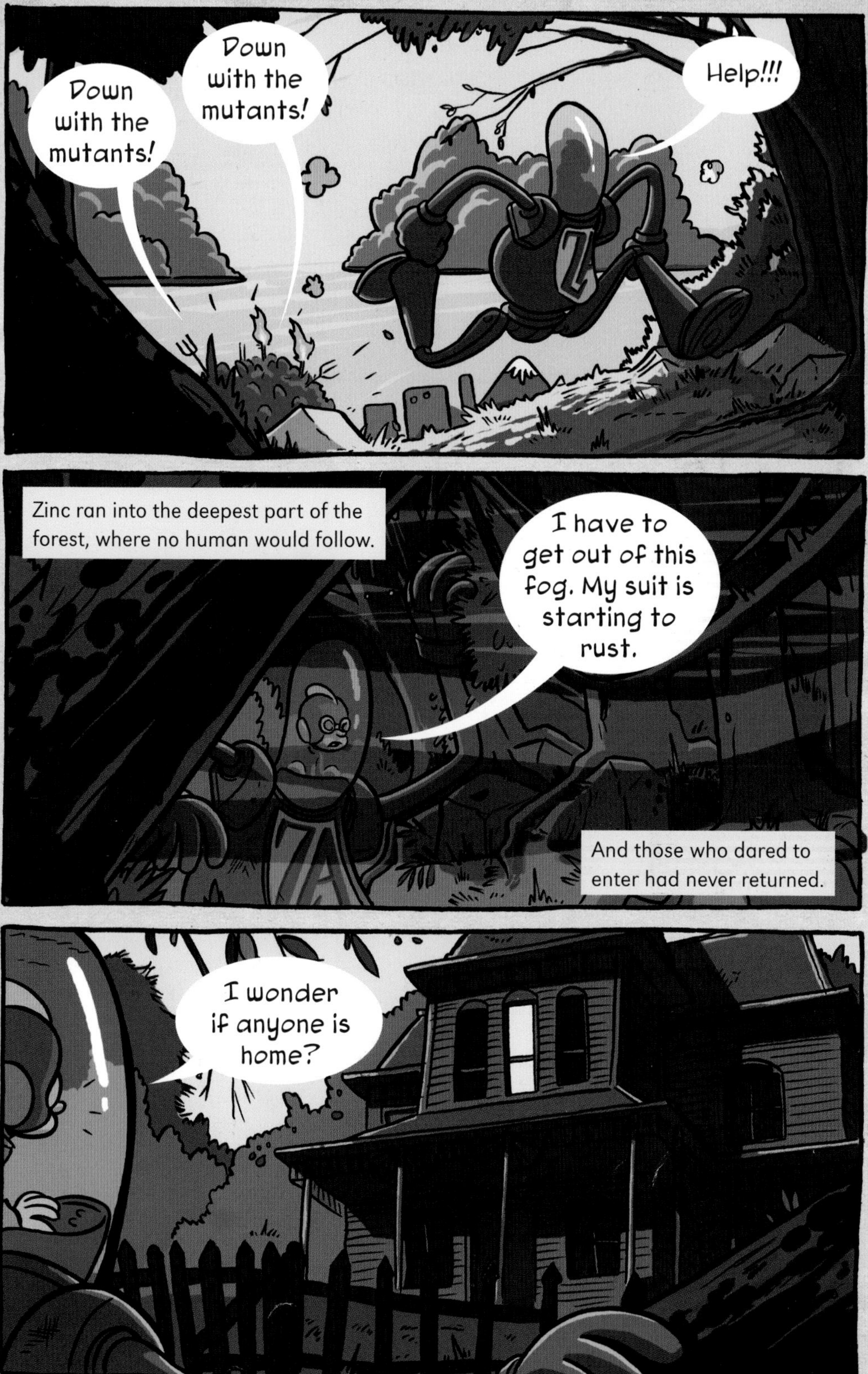
Down with the mutants!
Down with the mutants!
Help!!!
Zinc ran into the deepest part of the forest, where no human would follow.
I have to get out of this fog. My suit is starting to rust.
And those who dared to enter had never returned.
I wonder if anyone is home?

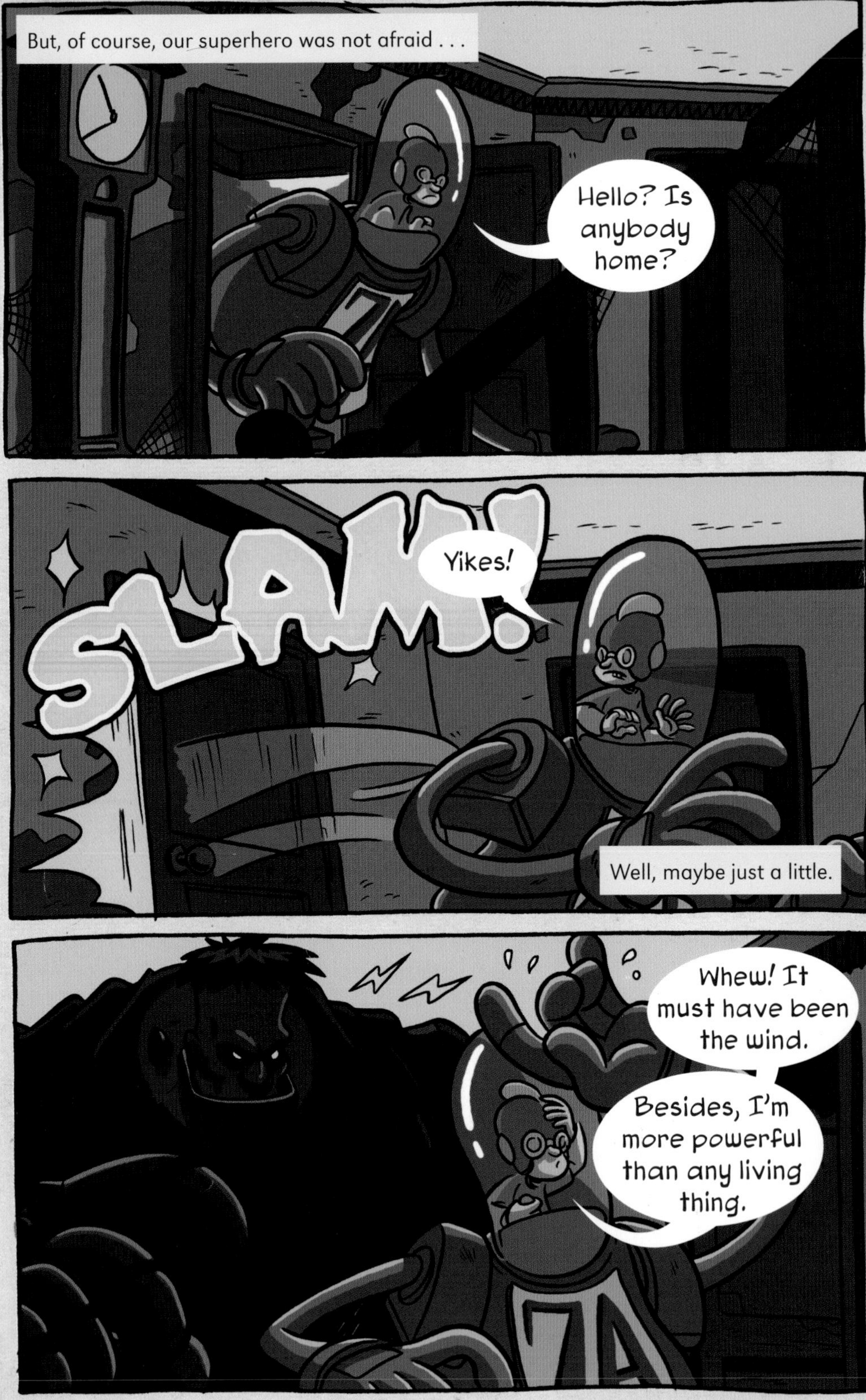
But, of course, our superhero was not afraid . . .
Hello? Is anybody home?
SLAM!
Yikes!
Well, maybe just a little.
Whew! It must have been the wind.
Besides, I'm more powerful than any living thing.

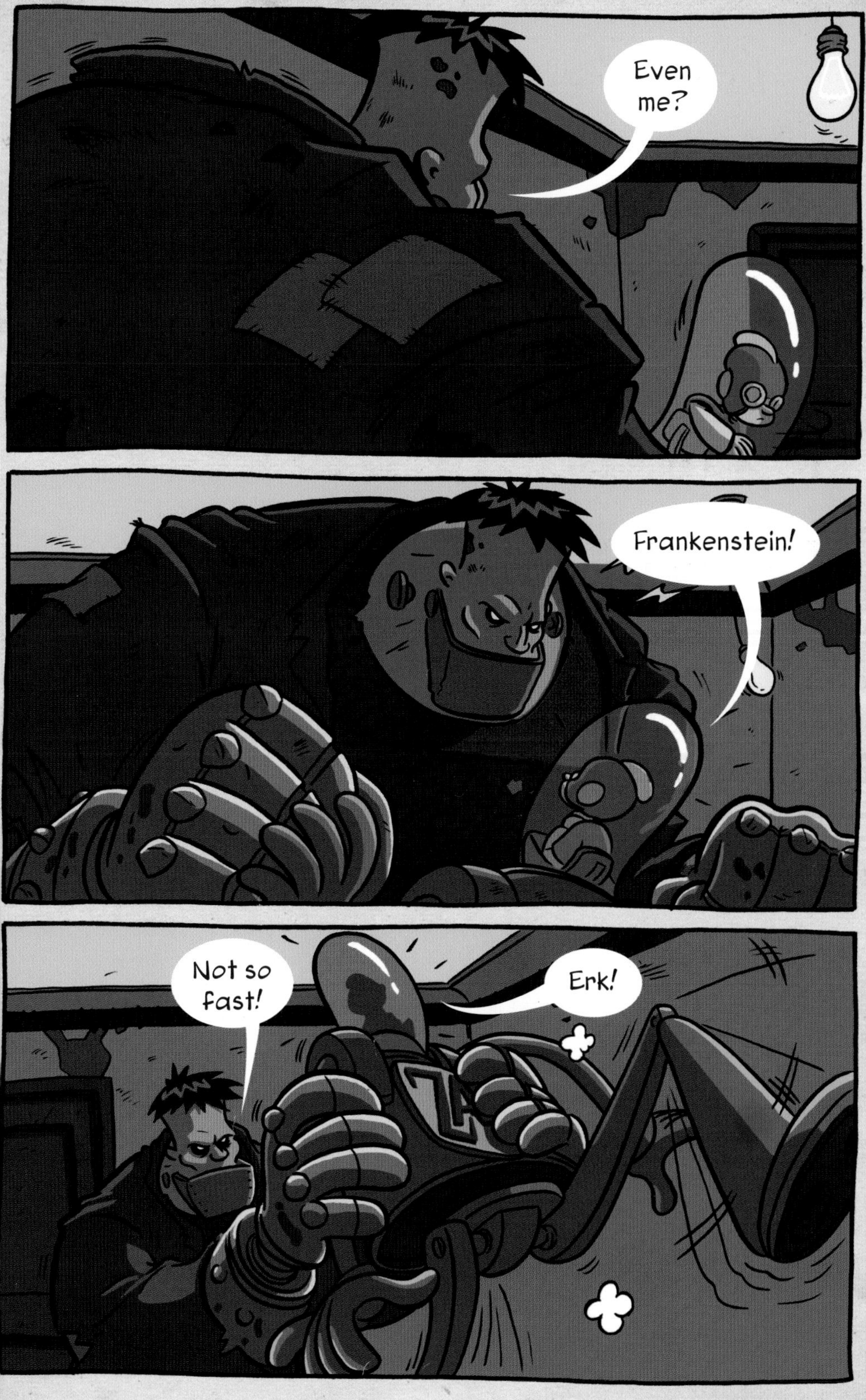
Even me?
Frankenstein!
Not so fast!
Erk!

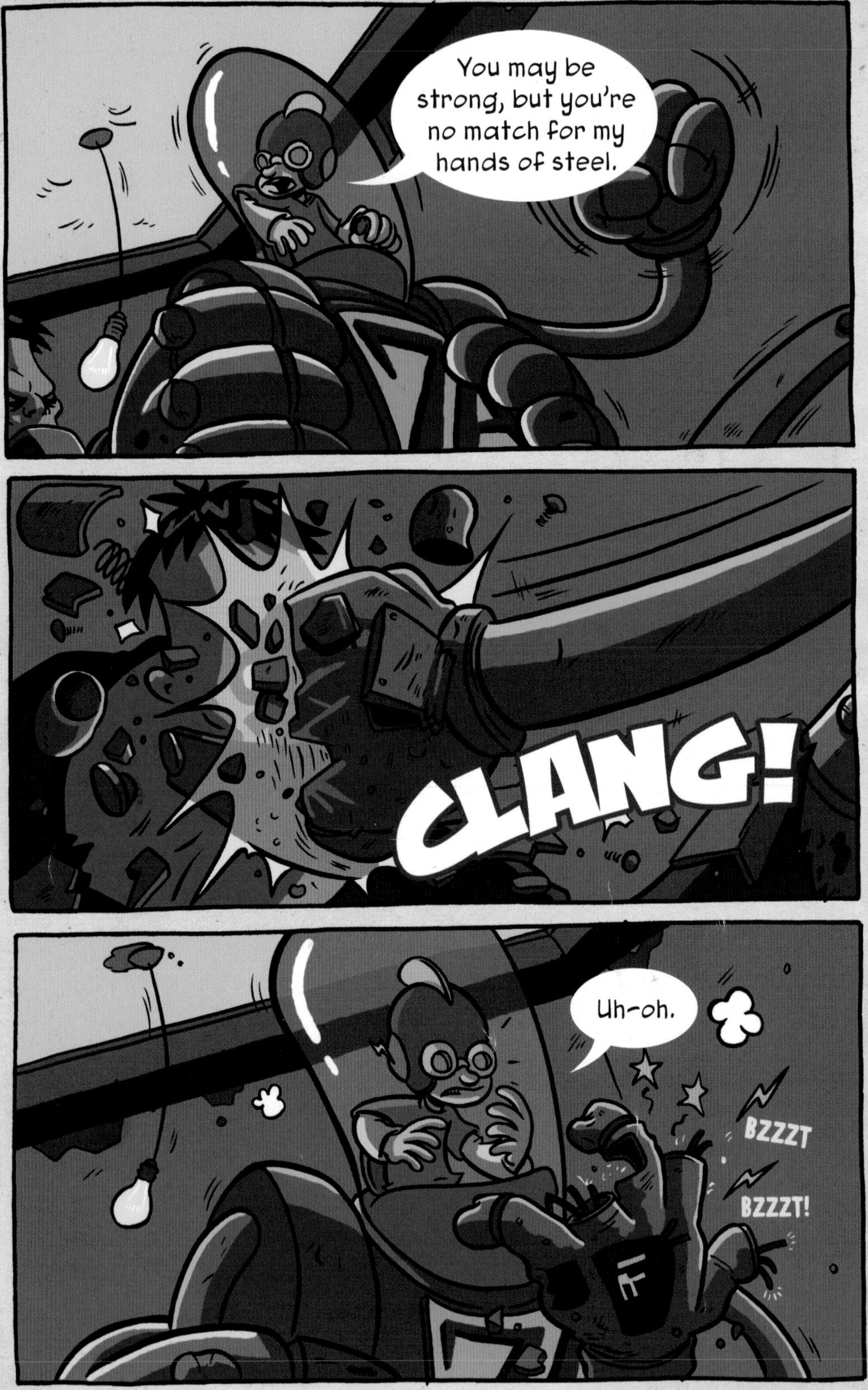
You may be strong, but you're no match for my hands of steel.
CLANG!
Uh-oh.
BZZZT
BZZZT!

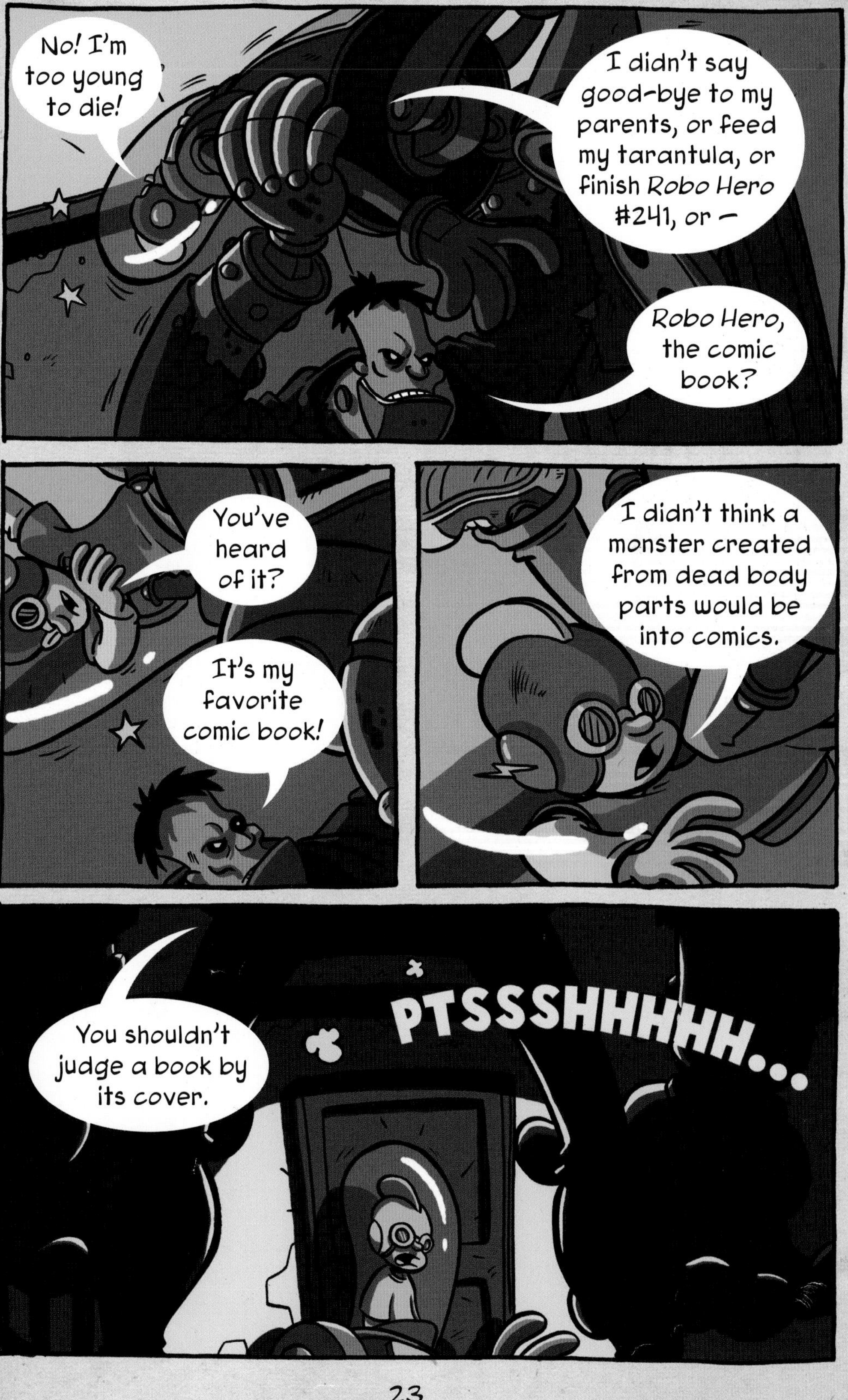
No! I'm too young to die!
I didn't say good-bye to my parents, or feed my tarantula, or finish *Robo Hero* #241, or —
Robo Hero, the comic book?
You've heard of it?
It's my favorite comic book!
I didn't think a monster created from dead body parts would be into comics.
You shouldn't judge a book by its cover.
PTSSSHHHHH...

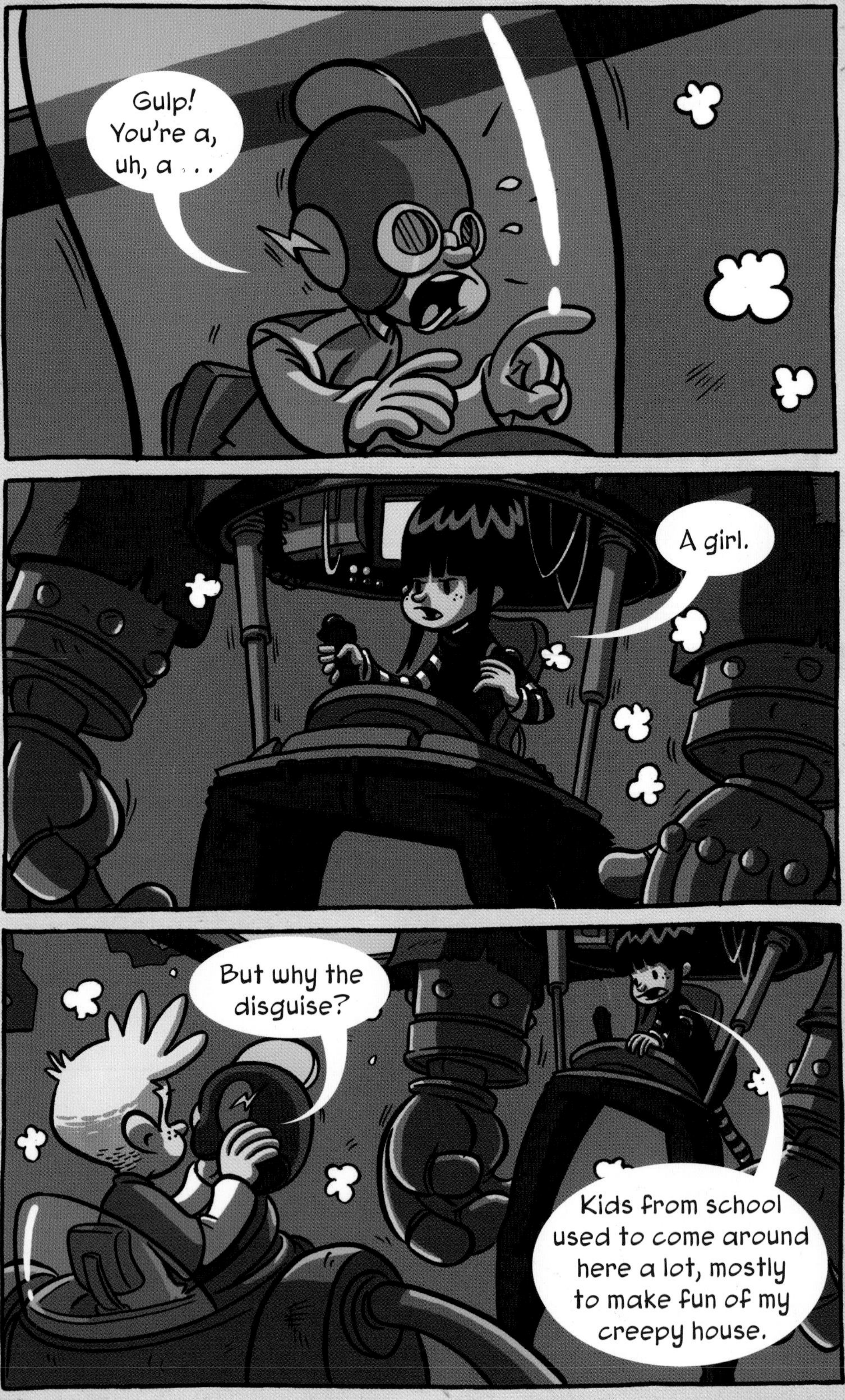
Gulp! You're a, uh, a . . .
A girl.
But why the disguise?
Kids from school used to come around here a lot, mostly to make fun of my creepy house.

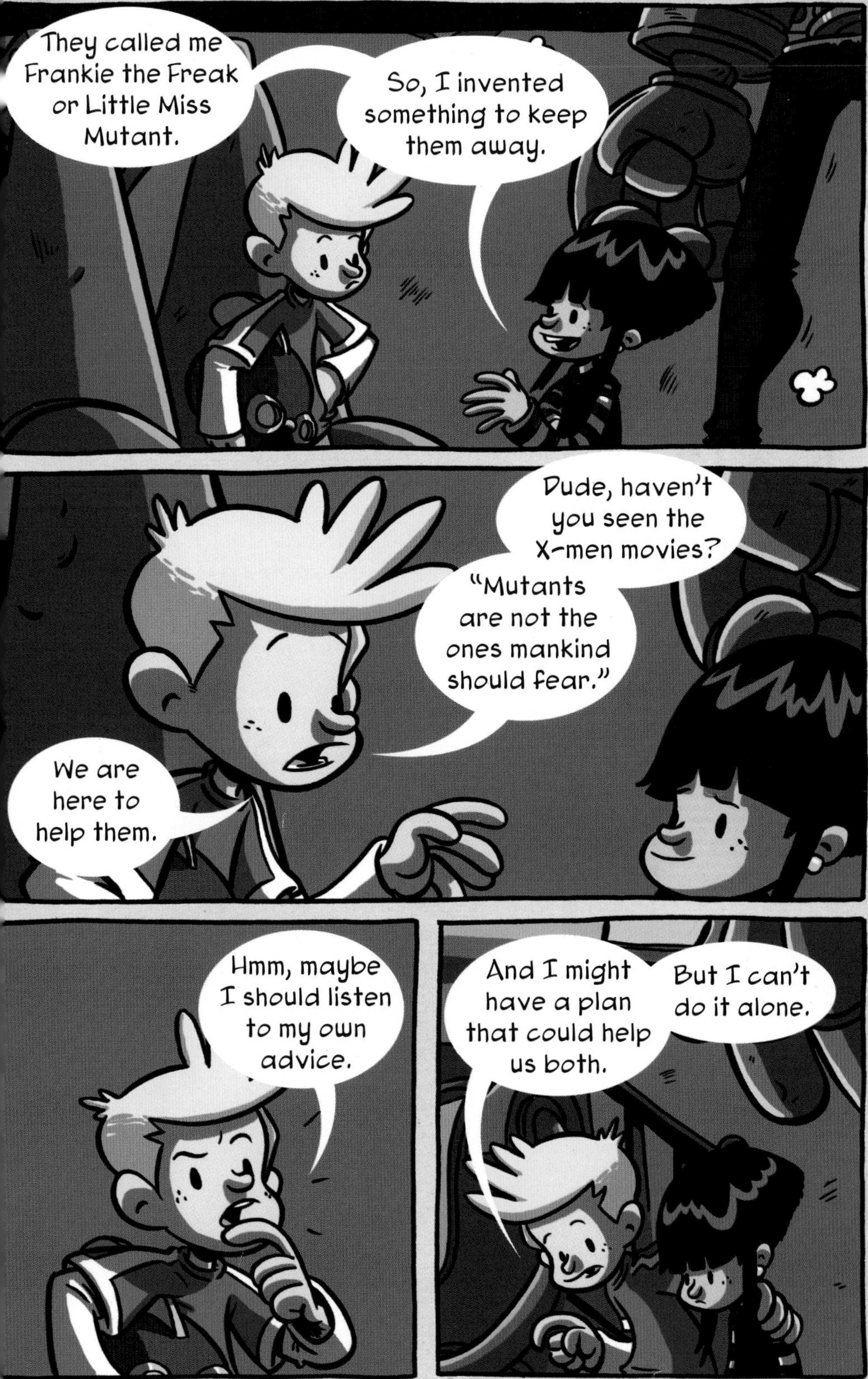
They called me Frankie the Freak or Little Miss Mutant.
So, I invented something to keep them away.
Dude, haven't you seen the X-men movies?
"Mutants are not the ones mankind should fear."
We are here to help them.
Hmm, maybe I should listen to my own advice.
And I might have a plan that could help us both.
But I can't do it alone.

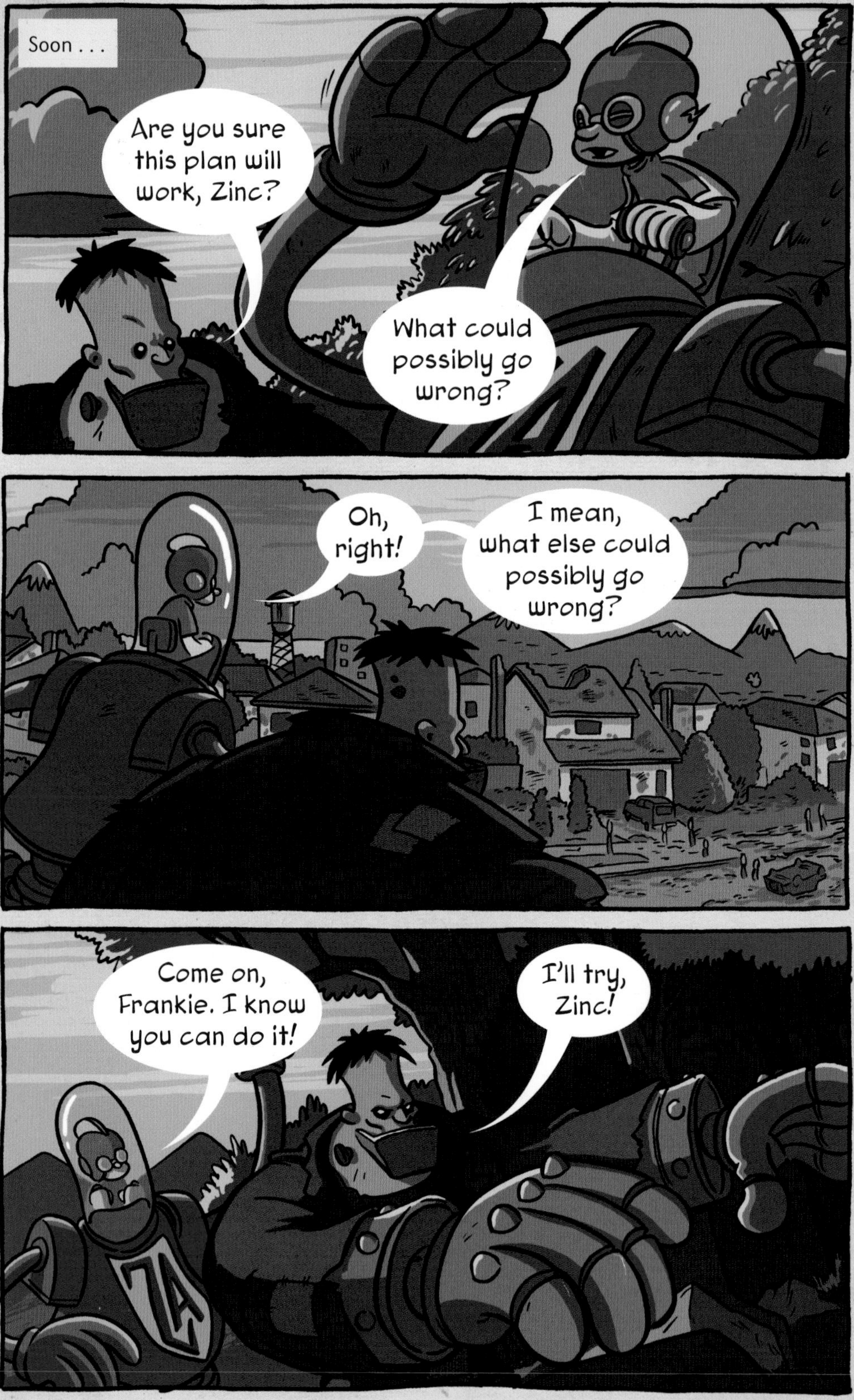
Soon . . .
Are you sure this plan will work, Zinc?
What could possibly go wrong?
Oh, right!
I mean, what else could possibly go wrong?
Come on, Frankie. I know you can do it!
I'll try, Zinc!

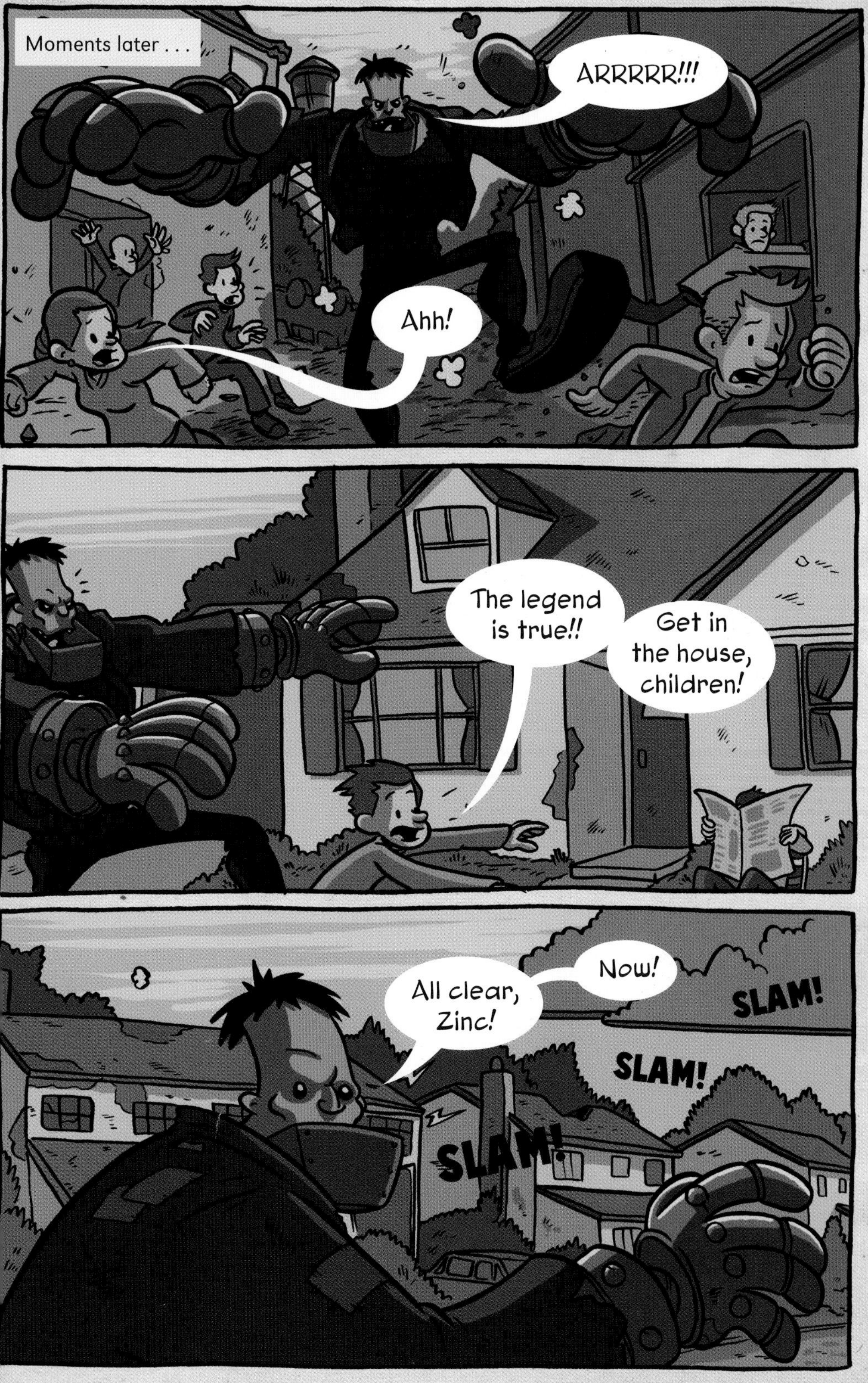
Moments later . . .
ARRRRR!!!
Ahh!
The legend is true!!
Get in the house, children!
All clear, Zinc!
Now!
SLAM!
SLAM!
SLAM!

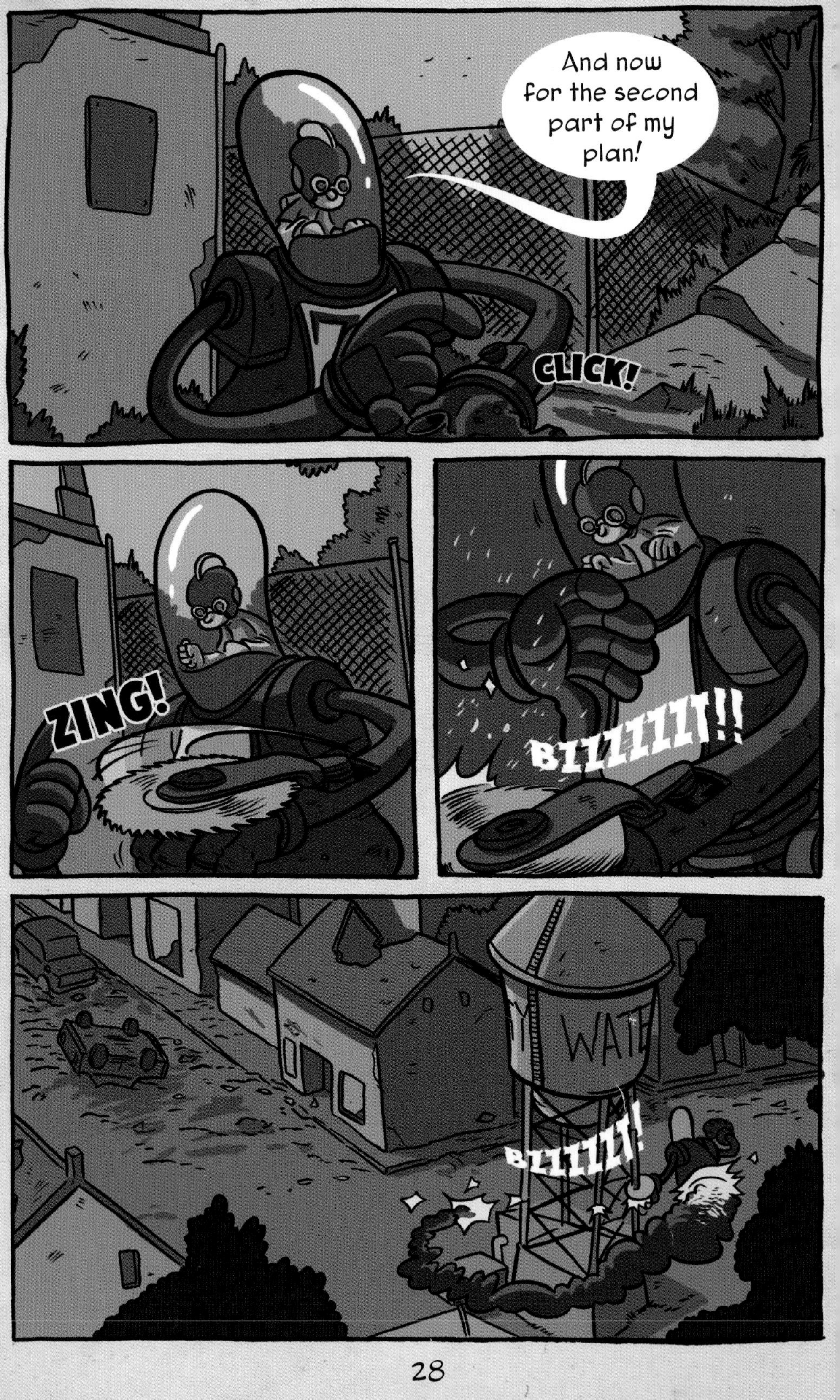
And now for the second part of my plan!
CLICK!
ZING!
BZZZZZZT!!
BZZZZT!

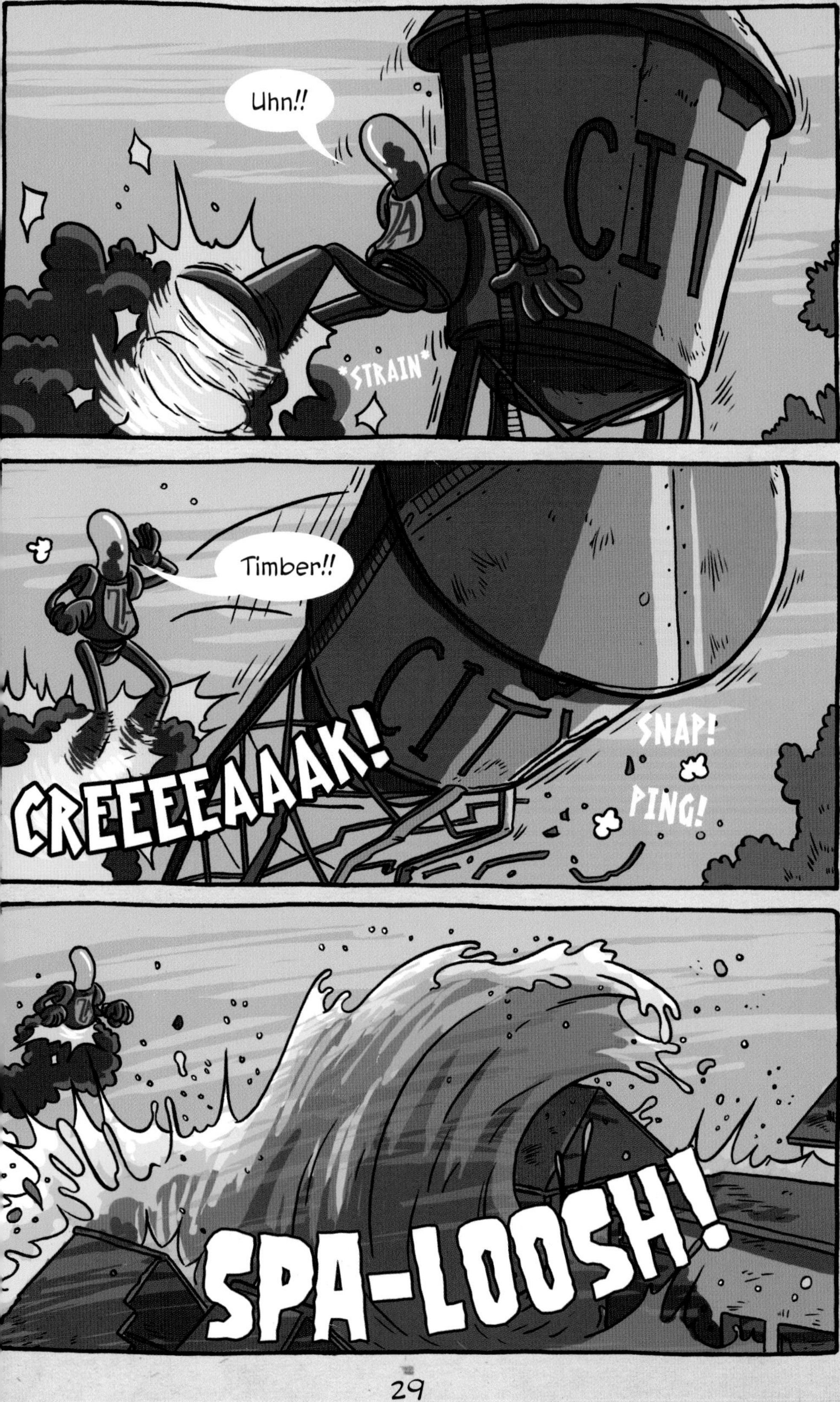
Uhn!!
STRAIN
CIT
Timber!!
CIT
CREEEEAAAK!
SNAP!
PING!
SPA-LOOSH!

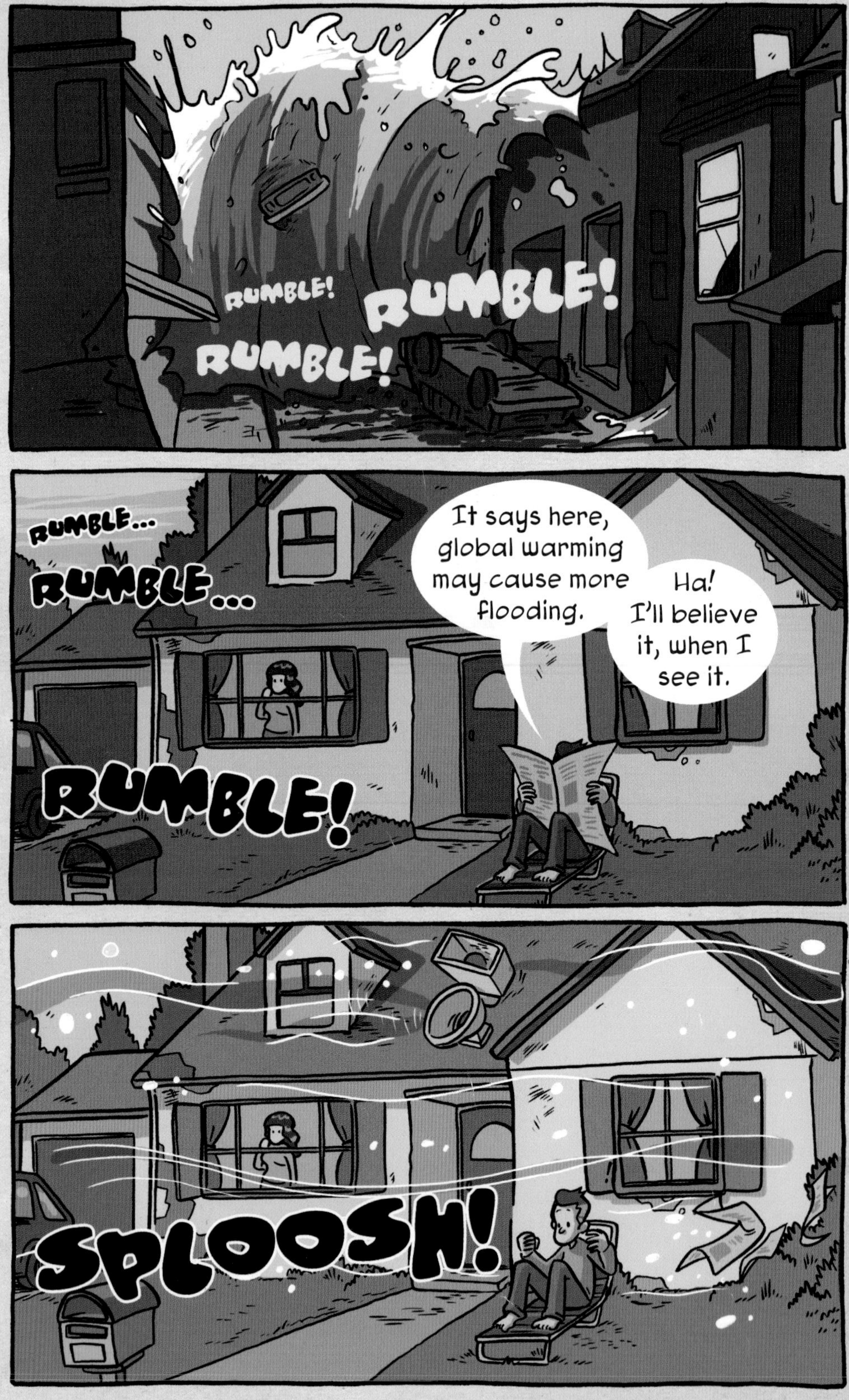
RUMBLE!
RUMBLE!
RUMBLE!
RUMBLE...
RUMBLE...
It says here, global warming may cause more flooding.
Ha! I'll believe it, when I see it.
RUMBLE!
SPLOOSH!

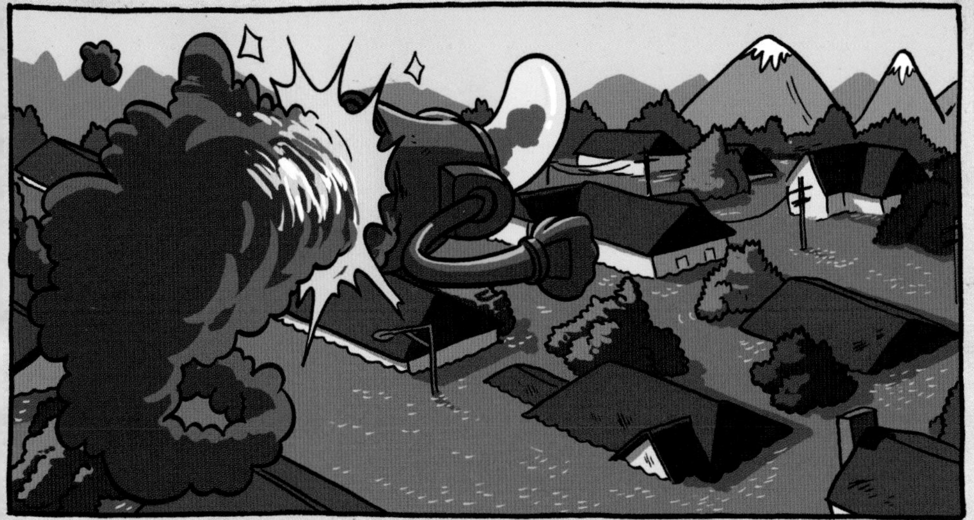

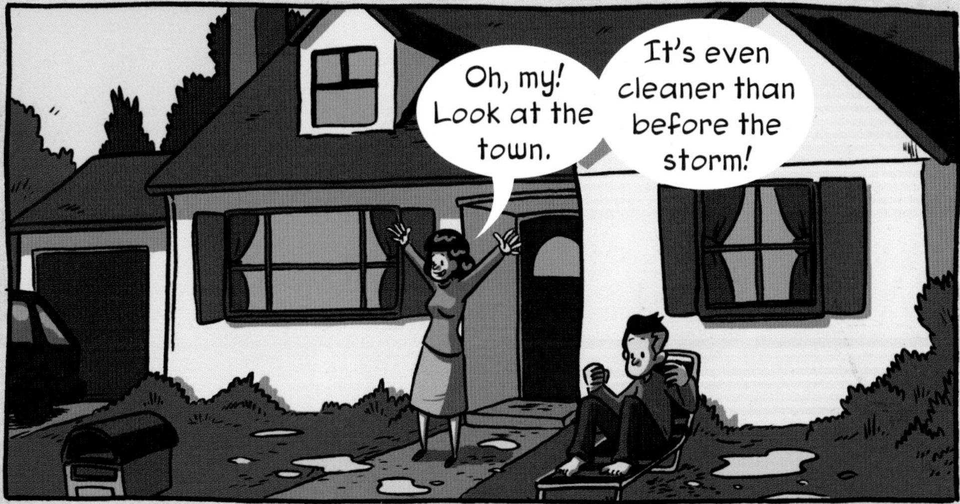
Oh, my! Look at the town.
It's even cleaner than before the storm!

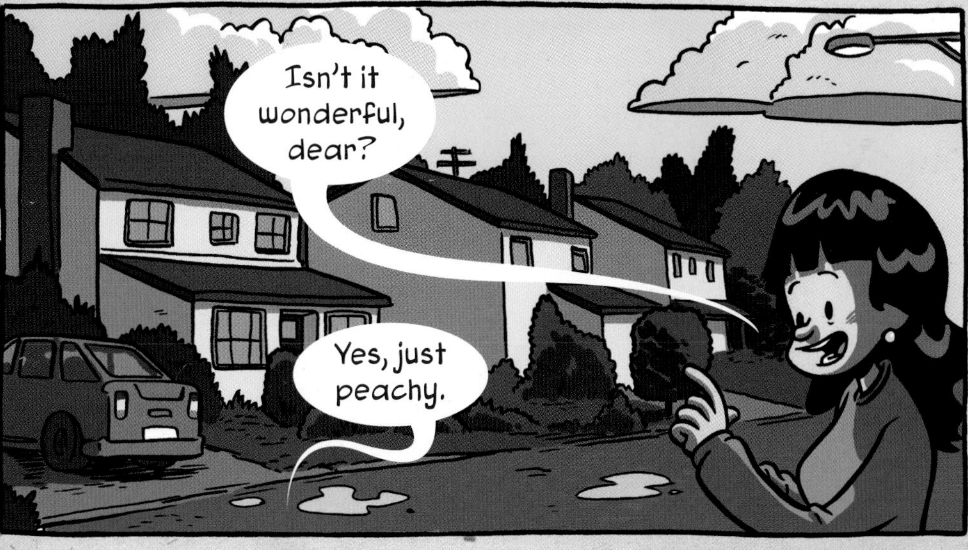
Isn't it wonderful, dear?
Yes, just peachy.

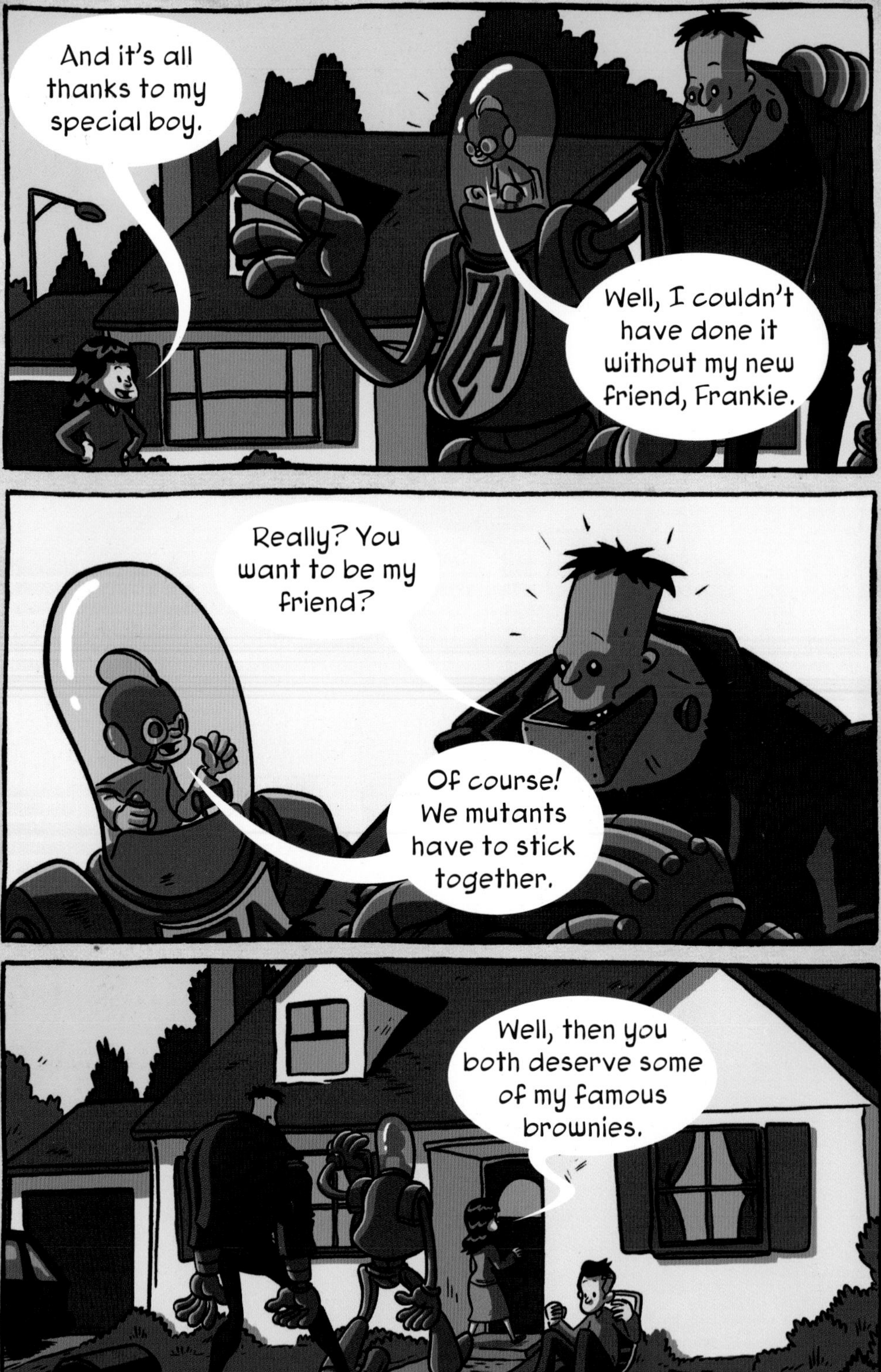
And it's all thanks to my special boy.
Well, I couldn't have done it without my new friend, Frankie.
Really? You want to be my friend?
Of course! We mutants have to stick together.
Well, then you both deserve some of my famous brownies.

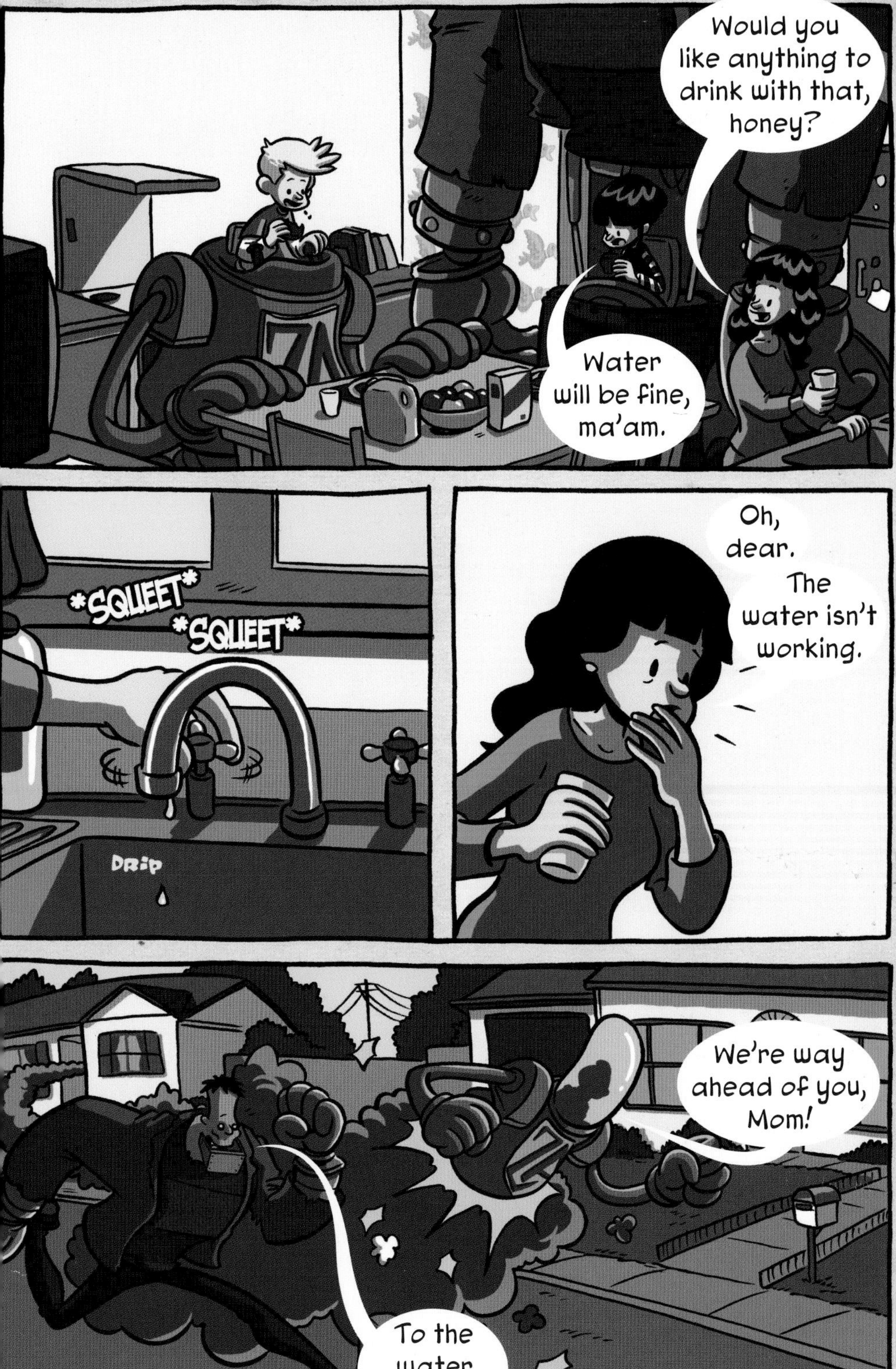
Would you like anything to drink with that, honey?
Water will be fine, ma'am.
SQUEET
SQUEET
DRIP
Oh, dear.
The water isn't working.
We're way ahead of you, Mom!
To the water tower!

About the Author

Donald Lemke works as a children's book editor and pursues a master's degree in publishing from Hamline University in St. Paul, Minnesota. He has written a variety of children's books and graphic novels. Most recently, he wrote *Captured Off Guard*, a World War II story, and a graphic novelization of *Gulliver's Travels*, both of which were selected by the Junior Library Guild.

About the Illustrator

Douglas Holgate is a freelance illustrator from Melbourne, Australia. His work has been published all around the world by Random House, Simon and Schuster, the *New Yorker* magazine, and Image Comics. His award-winning comic "Laika" appears in the acclaimed comic collection *Flight, Volume Two*.

Glossary

angry mob (ANG-gree MOB)—a large group of people using force to get what they want

cower (KOW-uhr)—to hide in fear or shame

heroic (hi-ROH-ik)—very brave or daring

force (FORSS)— the power behind the movement of something

innocent (IN-uh-suhnt)—not guilty, or unworthy of punishment

legend (LEJ-uhnd)—a story from long ago

miniature (MIN-ee-uh-chur)—smaller than the usual size

reverse (ri-VURSS)—change to the opposite position or path

rotating (ROH-tate-ing)—turning around like a wheel in a pattern

thruster (THRUHST-ur)—an object that causes forward or upward force

More About Frankenstein

The original novel about Frankenstein was published in 1818 by Mary Shelley. She was just 19 years old!

Shelley's name didn't appear on the first edition of *Frankenstein*. It wasn't on the novel until the second edition was printed in 1823.

In Mary Shelley's novel, the monster was not called Frankenstein. In fact, Shelley never named the monster.

In the novel, Doctor Victor Frankenstein is the mad scientist who gives the monster life. Some historians believe that Shelley based her mad scientist on the real-life physician, Johann Konrad Dippel of Germany.

Dippel was born and continued to live in Castle Frankenstein in Germany until his death in 1734. An annual Halloween party is now held at what remains of the 800-year-old castle.

The first film about the monster Frankenstein was 12 minutes long. It was shown in 1910. Like other films during this time, the movie didn't have any sound.

The modern version of Frankenstein comes from the 1931 *Frankenstein* film. Many sequels have stemmed from the movie, including *Bride of Frankenstein*, *Son of Frankenstein*, and *Ghost of Frankenstein.*

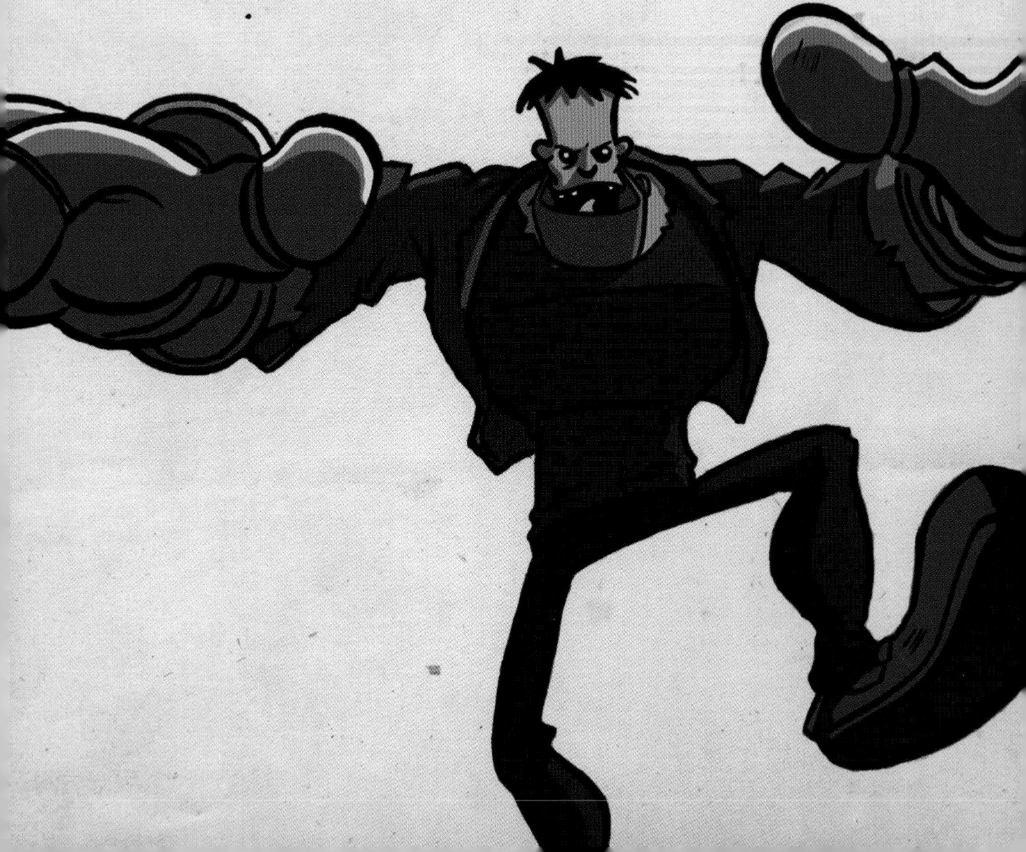

Discussion Questions

1. Zinc Alloy was trying to help, but his plan didn't work. Was it fair for the entire town to turn against him?

2. Zinc Alloy and Frankenstein are really just normal kids who dress up. If you could be any superhero, who would you be and why?

3. Both Zack and Frankie were teased at school. Have you ever been teased? How did that make you feel?